COMANCHE CROSSING

G. CLIFTON WISLER

PaperJacks LTD.

TORONTO NEW YORK

AN ORIGINAL

PaperJacks

COMANCHE CROSSING

PaperJacks LTD

330 STEELCASE RD. E., MARKHAM, ONT. L3R 2M1
210 FIFTH AVE., NEW YORK, N.Y. 10010

PaperJacks edition published June 1987

ISBN 0-7701-0626-9

Printed in the USA

Through the middle of the creek rode a single warrior, his arm holding high a bright yellow shield marked with a black band.

"Black Hand," Whit mumbled, waving Tom along at the head of the horses. Whit himself hung back, watched Black Hand cut off a dozen animals from the stampede, then head after more.

There was something unearthly about that Indian. Nothing, not the shooting or the shouting or the terrified cries of his injured comrades, seemed to affect him. It was impossible to see anything clearly in the dust and darkness, but even so Whit felt the eyes of that Indian, the bitter hatred burning like fire through the confusion.

"Ahhh-ayy-wha-cotayy!" Black Hand seemed to be screaming. Whit recognized the fury in the words, though he had no idea of their meaning. In those words rested the same pain, the same anguish that always filled a man who had lost something dear to him.

"These are my horses," the words seemed to declare. "This is my land! You have no right to take it from me!"

Yes, we're alike, Black Hand, Whit thought as he saw Coley and Ed ride past at the rear of the herd. Yes, I know how you feel. It's not so different from any war, though. Soldiers may be alike, but only one side can win, only one of us can call this place our own. And one of us must leave . . . or die.

IT BECAME A TEST OF WILLS

COMANCHE CROSSING

Chapter One

Texas was golden green. Spring rains had come early and stayed late that year. The rolling hills cut by the Trinity River were clothed in blankets of wild flowers. Bluebonnets and daisies intertwined with those strange yellow and red concoctions someone had named Indian paintbrushes. The river ran deep and swift, and there was a sweet smell to the land, a milk-and-honey kind of promise that would be gone come October.

The midafternoon sun was blazing down, and

nothing was stirring. Occasionally a maverick longhorn would saunter down to the river for a drink. Now and then a deer would venture from the safety of a thicket to chew the soft meadow grass. But it was too hot for exertion. Even the rattlesnakes sought shelter.

Down by the willows, where the catfish collected in a deep pool, a crow kept vigil over its territory. The bird cried out a challenge as something moved through the tall buffalo grass just beyond a great limestone boulder.

"Quiet, crow!" a man yelled. He hurled a small pebble toward the bird to show he meant business. The crow flew off into the low branches of a post oak across the river, crying out defiantly at the intruder. The man stumbled on, leading a fine chestnut stallion toward the river.

"It's been a long time," the man said, leaving his horse to drink as he stared across the river at a familiar hillside. "I used to catch the biggest river cats you ever did see under those willows."

There was no one there to hear the words, so they rolled around in the heavy summer air until they were forgotten. The man took off his dusty hat and scratched a head of dirty blond hair.

"Eight long years," he mumbled. "Seems only yesterday I was swimming in this river."

It wasn't yesterday, though. The river was swollen and deep, the land overgrown with wild flowers and cactus. And there were few traces of the cornfields which had straddled the Trinity years before.

"Things change," he whispered, glancing down at the dust which caked the trousers he'd bought only three weeks before in Kansas. "You look a little different yourself."

It was true. Whit Macomb was twenty-seven now, tanned and hard in a way no one who'd known him as a boy would have believed possible. He'd been straighter then, not all bent and broken. He hadn't had the scar on his forehead or the scraggly beard before. Some had called him handsome. Lucy Brown, for one. There was too much hardness now, too many wrinkles and aches and tears.

Kneeling down, Whit cupped his hands, dipped them in the river and drew the water to his mouth. The cool liquid soothed his parched throat, and for the first time a smile came to his lips. There was a taste of home in that water. More than once that taste had come to him in a dream, a vision of returning to a place full of peace and fresh-baked bread, warm beds and soft shoulders. Those were the things Whit Macomb missed the most.

He stood up and stroked the nose of his horse. It wasn't every animal that could carry a man across half of Kansas, through the Indian Nations and down from Red River Crossing in three weeks. Now Whit was home at last, and there would be days of soft grass and easy living ahead.

"Come on, boy," he coaxed, leading the horse along the bank to where an ancient post oak stood. Stepping three paces beyond, Whit then led the horse across the river, using the same path crossed by man and beast since the waters of the Trinity first churned through the land.

Not many knew the ford. The Comanches did. It was where their war parties crossed the river when they attacked the settlements back in the fifties. Whit had been little more than a boy then. He was thirteen the year the Indians burned the farm. He rubbed the withered left hand that had been bent and half useless ever since he'd touched a red-hot ramrod the morning after the raid.

Those last few years before the war the Comanches had pretty much left people alone. The government set up an agency at Fort Belknap for a time. Then in the summer of '59 the First Infantry, or rather a company of it anyway, had escorted the last of the agency Comanches across the Red River into the Nations.

Whit remembered that journey. He'd been supplying Mr. Kelp, one of the Indian agents, with beef. The army had been short on experienced horsemen, and few objections had been raised when Whit volunteered to go along. Those Comanches had been calm, not at all like the ones who'd raided livestock and burned farms only a couple of years earlier.

As he led his horse from the river on the southern bank, Whit felt something cold grip his insides. The mud was torn up with sign. Dozens of horses had been through there only hours before. Most were unshod ponies.

"Indians?" he wondered, clutching the handle of the Colt revolver he wore on his hip. "No, must be that old Ruben's gone, and there's no one to do the shoeing."

More likely no iron for shoes, he thought as he topped a low ridge and stared at the valley which stretched from old Hadley's Spring to the river. Iron had been hard to come by in the South following the capture of New Orleans. Most places still hadn't caught up with prewar trade, and it was five long years since the armistice had been signed.

Whit shook some of the dampness from his trouser legs and mounted the stallion. As he urged the horse into a slow trot, he nodded to the tall white oak standing atop a hill fifty feet or so down the trail.

Marty's favorite swimming hole lay where the white oak draped its branches over the river. It was deep there, and shady even on the hottest August afternoons. As Whit gazed at the river, he was half tempted to shed his dusty clothes and jump in.

"Mama never took to filthy men," he mumbled. There might even be a chance to shave off the stubble that had appeared in the three days since he'd camped with the Circle T boys up the trail. It wasn't in him to delay his homecoming another minute, though.

Whit urged his horse onward. A gentle rise blocked the view of the house from the river. It had been Whit's father's idea to shield the farm buildings from bands of marauding Comanches making the river crossing. As it turned out, that hadn't meant much. By the time an Indian was half grown, he could sniff out a white man's cook fires.

Whit's heart raced as he approached the crest of the hill.

"Katie! Marty! Mama! I'm back!" he cried out.

No answer came. The words echoed back at him in an unearthly taunt. And as he continued, he discovered what remained of the house lying in ruins, an ugly charcoal scar on the land.

To Whit's left stood one wall of the barn. The

rest had collapsed, forming a mound of blackened timbers. The toolshed he and his brother Marty had built the summer before the war was also gone.

Whit rolled out of the saddle and left his horse to graze on the high grass that had overgrown the farmyard. Not so much as a feather survived from the three dozen plump chickens he remembered feeding that last morning before leaving the valley. No sign of livestock . . . of people. . . . Not even a hint of some passing horse could be located near the house.

It's been a long time since anyone's been here, he told himself. Years.

The realization hollowed out his insides. It was hard to breathe without trembling. He wasn't exactly angry. There'd been too much hatred that hard winter of '58 when he'd brought his father's body home, all the life crushed out of it by a Comanche war club. No, it was more than anger.

"Mama?" he whispered, searching the encroaching trees for some hint of the warm face he'd dreamed of being there. All the way from the Dakotas Whit had pictured the surprise that would flood her face, how warm he'd feel when they embraced again. He hadn't even written.

Whit stumbled toward the house, staring at the ashes of what had once been home. Over on the east side, where the room he'd shared with Marty had stood, something flashed in the sunlight. He walked over and picked up the twisted barrel of an ancient flintlock rifle.

"I killed a wolf with that gun," he mumbled, recalling the autumn when his father had gone to

Fort Belknap to do some carpentry work for the army. Whit had been twelve. He'd stalked that wolf for two days, then killed it with a single shot.

He dropped the barrel and stepped forward. Across the way rested the metal hinges and charred framework of his sister Katie's hope chest.

"God, let them be safe," Whit prayed, staring overhead at the brilliant summer sun. "The rest doesn't matter so long as they're alive."

That wasn't quite true. The burning, well, it did matter. But a house could be rebuilt. Hadn't they done it before, and in the dead of winter after the Comanches had killed his father? Whit would have been willing to stay in Jacksboro, working for old Ruben Gaines.

Not Mama, though, Whit remembered. She put up a fight. It wasn't any ordinary woman could raise three kids, fight off Indians, and still get a crop in at harvest time.

Whit rubbed a tear from his eye and stared again at the remains of the house. It wasn't a time for crying. No, his father had said that often enough.

"Ashes to ashes," old Reverend Henriks had said at the burying. Everything returned to the earth in its turn. First it had been his father. This time it was the farm.

"Even the dreams die, huh, Papa?" Whit whispered to the wind.

Even now his father's words seemed to fill the place. There was to have been another barn, fifty more acres cleared for corn. A hundred horses, a herd of cattle. . . . The house was to have a porch, new curtains, a fresh coat of paint each spring.

Well, they had painted once, in '59, when Ruben had ordered more paint than he'd needed for the stable in town.

"Even the dreams die," Whit said again, closing his eyes so he wouldn't have to see the house anymore. But it didn't go away. And after a few minutes he opened his eyelids and glanced around for his horse.

"We can camp at Hadley's Spring," Whit told the stallion. He then put his withered left hand on the saddle horn and pulled himself onto the horse's back.

Hadley's Spring formed a little pond as it spilled out of a rocky gorge two miles west of the farmhouse. It was named for an old frontiersman who'd found the place while fleeing a Kiowa war party. It probably was a better site for the house, and Whit had considered moving the family there. If the war hadn't broken out, he likely would've married Lucy Brown. They could have had their home there, with all the good timber on the mountain and close to six hundred acres for cattle and horses.

It was a good place for thinking, Hadley's Spring. He'd taken Marty up there after their father'd died, more to think out the future than to give any profound words of advice to his brother. But it turned out a good time, the night they'd stayed up there all alone. Whit went back feeling more of a man.

The place hadn't changed much. With the Trinity so close, the Comanches didn't need water from the spring. And there wasn't anything there to steal or burn. Whit slid down from the saddle and began tending to his horse. The animal had been ridden hard, and now there wouldn't be a chance to rest. Tomorrow they'd be riding into Jacksboro.

As night began to fall, Whit spread out his blankets and heated a tin of beans. There was some bread left from the little trading post at Red River Crossing, and he nibbled at it. It was a far cry from beef stew or fried chicken. He didn't really have much appetite, though.

The night winds brought a strange chill to the land, uncommon for late summer. It rarely got cool before October, and the change was just another reminder to Whit of how different things were. The stars overhead appeared distant, somehow foreign, and he climbed into his blankets early.

He found little rest, though. The wind continued to whine through the post oaks, and the owls were restless. Across the river a lone wolf howled at the moon, a yellow-white circle cut by a feathery cloud.

On toward midnight Whit heard a horse. It was almost silent, and only a man who'd spent the last seven years of his life alternately chasing and being chased by Cheyenne and Sioux would have noticed. But the sound was there, a slight rustle of leaves and a splash in the river.

Whit said nothing. He reached for the shiny Henry rifle wrapped in a buffalo hide beside his saddle. Without thinking, he slid the bullets into the magazine. Then he crept forward, inching his way to the edge of the clearing that stood at the foot of the gorge.

The wolf howled again, sending shivers down Whit's spine. The night wind bit through him, but he never flinched. There, below him in the moonlight, stood a single Indian, tall and straight like a chief's coup stick. The man's eyes burned in the faint light. His bare chest was marked with streaks of red and yellow paint. On the rump of his pony was a large black hand, painted warrior fashion.

The markings on the Indian's face, the beadwork on his vest, and the band across his forehead spelled only one thing. Comanche. Whit ground his teeth as the Indian defiantly shouted words Whit couldn't understand. Their meaning became clear enough, though, when the warrior gestured wildly in the direction of the burned-out shell of a house.

It was more than Whit could stand. He walked out from the protection of the trees and held the rifle in his strong right hand.

"No, this is my place!" Whit shouted. "And it's me that's going to do the killing from now on!"

The words echoed through the clearing as if spoken by a hundred men. The Comanche moved back. The wolf was joined by another, and another. Soon the hillside was alive with howling, and the wind stirred. A storm was brewing to the west.

Whit's heart burned with anger, but he wasn't sure of his aim. To miss was to invite retaliation. No, if there was one thing the war had taught him, it was to never start anything you're not prepared to finish then and there. It was why they'd failed at Shiloh, at Corinth. And in the end it was why they'd had to surrender Vicksburg.

"Our time will come," Whit told the moon and the wolves and the midnight wind.

A streak of lightning flashed across the sky, and it started to rain. Before he raced to get his poncho, Whit glanced at the clearing. The Comanche had vanished. The skies emptied themselves then, and Whit stumbled back to the spring. It would be a wet and miserable night.

Chapter Two

It was a weary Whit Macomb who headed into Jacksboro that next morning. The storm lasted most of the night, and little sleep had come to him. There were too many questions in his mind, too many answers waiting for him in town.

From the Macomb Farm on the West Fork of the Trinity to where the town of Jacksboro nestled against the meandering waters of Lost Creek lay some ten miles of rolling hills and winding creeks. There was a trail worn by time from the little trading post of Buffalo Springs south to Jacksboro, and Whit wove his way across the two low sandstone ridges which stood between Hadley's Spring and the point where the primitive road touched the edge of the farm's southeastern boundary.

Jack County was hard country. The flatlands were speckled with sagebrush and prickly pear. Out past the river only occasional stands of blackjack and post oaks broke the monotony of the Texas plain. Vast valleys of buffalo grass spread out westward. It was once prime range for herds of buffalo, home for the bands of Comanche and Kiowa hunters who followed the migrations of the great hairy beasts.

Before the war, small farms provided a meager living along the Trinity. As Whit made his way to town, he noticed more than one black scar which marked the home of some former friend and neighbor.

It was late afternoon when he reached Jacksboro. The town, too, had changed. The huddle of wooden buildings that spread out along the road to Fort Belknap had expanded. In addition, soldiers were busy constructing a line of wooden picket buildings near the south bank of Lost Creek a mile from the center of town.

The streets of Jacksboro were deserted except for a cluster of off-duty blue-coated soldiers. Whit had seen too many of them in the Dakotas and later in Kansas for it to disturb him much. Some of the townspeople eyed them with suspicion, though, and one woman walking near the mercantile detoured out of her way to avoid the group.

Whit paused a minute as he passed the Methodist

church. His father was buried in the churchyard there, and he thought to stop a minute. But before he could turn his horse in that direction, he heard someone call out his name.

"Whit?" a deep voice called out again. "Whit Macomb?"

No sooner were the words uttered than a burly man of near fifty charged out of nowhere and close to pulled Whit right off his horse.

Whit trembled as he managed to get to the ground. All the disappointment he felt the day before when he found the farm burned flew away that very instant. He swallowed a sigh and smiled at the old man.

"How are you, Ruben?" Whit asked.

"Fair. And how are you, Whit Macomb?"

"Just about home, I'd say," Whit replied, looking the old man over from chin to toe.

Ruben Gaines wasn't what you'd call a handsome sort of man. He was a half-century old now, and what hair remained on his head had turned white as February snow. There were wrinkles on his forehead, liver spots on his giant hands, but not a hint of infirmity.

"You look good, Ruben," Whit said, nodding.

"Don't look so bad yourself, boy," Ruben said, squeezing Whit's arms and lifting him into the air. "A mite thin, but what's there's solid enough to be from Jack County."

"I see you're still keeping horses."

"Twenty or so. And I do some smithing for the army. Don't know that I like working for all those Yanks, what with 'em killing Bowie Hayes and

Jack Lowery at Elkhorn Tavern, but they pay gold and silver."

"I'm glad you're still here, Ruben. So much has changed. It's good to stand here in front of your stable, smell the fire from the forge and the fresh hay."

"You used to spend a good bit of time in that hay, as I remember."

"That was a long time ago," Whit said, feeling a darkness come to his eyes as he recalled those happy days before the war when the farm was still there and a warm bed waited for him when the day's toil was done.

"You been out to the old place?" Ruben asked.

"Yes."

"Not much there anymore. I got some of your things in back. You know — the old saddle, that knife you brought back from the Belknap agency, some tintypes and the like. Katie left them here."

"What happened, Ruben?"

"What always happens round here. Comanches."

"And my family?"

"Fought off the worst of it. But you know your mama. Had to get into town every Sunday for services. While they were here, a dozen or so bucks hit the farm. Ran off all the stock, burned the barn. Your mama saved most everything out of the house, but Marty being just twelve, there wasn't much point to trying to start all over."

"So where are they?"

"Katie took herself a husband. They're down to Waco. Marty's there, too."

"And Mama?"

"Well, Whit, you know her heart was here. She wouldn't leave."

"Where is she?"

"She worked in the mercantile for a year. It was just before the surrender. She hadn't heard a word from you, only that you were at Vicksburg when it was taken."

"So?"

"She wasn't eating any too good, and I told her she ought to take it easier. One night she went to bed. Mrs. Gibbons found her next morning."

"Dead?"

"Passed on in her sleep. Oh, we had a real nice service for her. Near everyone in town turned out. Katie and Marty came back. It was just what she'd've wanted. Buried her beside your papa."

Whit gazed across the street at the churchyard. The hollow feeling returned, and he blinked away a tear.

"I'd've written you if I'd known how, Whit," Ruben said. "Didn't know where you were, what had happened to you. Tom Baker came back with his leg off, told how the Yanks took the Second Texas prisoner at Vicksburg. We never heard anything more."

"We were all paroled. Some went along home. I was exchanged. Served for a time in the cavalry up in Kentucky. Got myself captured again, taken to prison camp up north. They gave us our pardon on condition we go fight Indians in the Dakotas."

"I heard the Yanks were doing that."

"I thought not to go at first. But I figured I'd go crazy sitting around that prison camp, stinking to high heaven, with bad meat and stale bread to eat.

Besides, we knew the war was over after Vicksburg. I'd never been to the high country."

"You come by the scar up there?" Ruben asked, pointing to the thin white line which marked Whit's left temple.

"Powder River country. Almost lost my hair. Got a better one on my shoulder."

"I'd wager you gave better'n you took."

"Some might say so."

"I want you to tell me all about it, but I got to finish mending some harness for the stage. You got a place to stay?"

"Not yet."

"I'd think highly of it if you'd take the old room back of the stable."

"I'll consider it."

"Do that. Whit, why don't you come in and stable your horse? He looks full blown, and you're not much better yourself."

"That I'll do."

While Ruben went back to work, Whit took the saddle off the tired stallion and began washing the trail dust from the weary animal. As he began brushing the horse's coat, the fine chestnut coloring began to shine again.

"I could do that for you, mister," someone said as Whit stroked the animal's forehead.

"Just about finished," Whit answered, turning to face a blond-haired boy of about fourteen.

"He's got fine lines," the boy observed. "Had him long?"

"Few months. But we got to be good friends coming down from Kansas."

"Been on the cattle trail? Abilene? I'd really like

to be out on the range, raising my own dust and living the fine life."

"You know cattle?"

"I spent my whole growing up on a ranch. My daddy was a top man with a rope. That was before the war."

"Not much ranching around here now, I suppose."

"Nope," the boy said, looking at his toes.

"You two getting acquainted?" Ruben asked, walking over with the harness.

"A little," Whit said.

"Well, knowing you two like I do, I don't suppose either of you bothered to tell the other what your name is. Tom," the old man said, patting the boy on the back, "this is Whitman Macomb, best man with horses I ever knew. Whit, this is Tom Morgan. You remember Henry Morgan, used to run freight up from Fort Worth?"

"Sure," Whit replied, extending his hand so that young Tom Morgan could shake it. "I always thought highly of your father."

"Indians killed him three summers back," Tom whispered.

"Tom, this harness needs to go over to the stage office," Ruben said, passing over the harness. "You see it gets there."

"It will," Tom said. He pulled the heavy leather lines toward him and made his way out of the stable and on down the street.

"He's an orphan," Ruben explained to Whit. "Works like thunder."

Whit smiled. "Still taking in strays, I see. I

remember you took in another one a few years back."

"I never thought of you as a stray, Whit. You just needed a little cash to help your mama keep the farm going."

"I wasn't talking about the work, Ruben. I mean all the things you showed me about tending stock. All the other things, too."

"Such as?"

"How to be a man."

"Nobody ever had to show Whit Macomb that. You had more man in you at five years than a lot of people I know."

Whit warmed as Ruben reminded him of things they'd done together, hunting buffalo the spring of '58, tracking down a mountain lion two weeks before Whit left for the war.

"Ought to have been more happy times," Ruben said, putting a bearlike hand on Whit's shoulder. "Ought to've been."

"Papa used to talk like that," Whit remembered. "He always told me a man doesn't write his own life. He only lives it the best he can. I guess that's all there is to do, Ruben."

"I expect that's so."

"I guess maybe I ought to pay my respects to Mama and Papa before it gets dark. Reverend might wonder what I was doing around there after the sun goes down."

"Might at that."

"I'll be by later," Whit promised.

"Be watching for you, son."

Whit gave his horse a parting slap on the rump,

then walked across the street to the churchyard. He hadn't been there in years, but he could have located the graves blindfolded. Every Sunday they'd gone there, Whit leading his mother, Katie and Marty close behind. There'd always been a little prayer. Then his mother made each of them tell their father what they'd been up to since the week before.

A smile crossed Whit's lips as he recalled watching Marty squirm, then confess some devilment. It seemed worse than going before a hanging judge.

When Whit knelt beside the headstones which marked the graves of his parents, his smile disappeared. He said nothing, just touched the cold granite and remembered. In his heart he shared with them the pain and disappointment that had filled his life those terribly long, last eight years. Then he swallowed the sadness and stood up.

"I'll remember your dream, Papa," he whispered. "It won't die easy."

Chapter Three

The western horizon was lit with one of those sunsets people tell stories about. Every possible shade of yellow and orange splashed its way across the sky. An angry black thundercloud roared up in the center of it all, casting a vermilion tint onto the heavens. It was enough to take a man right out of himself.

Whit watched it for a time. Sunsets always reminded him of Texas. Many evenings those last few years as he'd made his way homeward, he'd dreamt of sitting on the porch, telling Marty about wolves and mountain cats and the turkey they'd shoot for Christmas dinner. Marty was grown now, and the porch never got built, but that didn't stop the dreaming.

It's what life's all about, Whit told himself. The dreams. It was what made a man better than himself. Those dreams had kept Whit going when the Sioux had them all half starved and near dead in that shambles of a fort on the Powder River. He'd never given up, not then or on the long way south across half the country.

Whit made his way down the street toward Lost Creek. He'd strolled there with Lucy Brown when they were young, holding her hand, feeling the warmth of her smile. Whit recalled staring at the moon and mapping out a future. But plans were no good. There was always a war or an Indian raid to turn everything upside down.

Lost Creek ran swiftly that evening. The night before's rains had made it muddy and deep. As he looked southward, he saw the fort. The work had stopped now. A hundred yards from the creek a large stone structure towered over two rows of barracks, rough, picket huts like those partially completed. Between the picket buildings was a square parade ground. Long lines of cone-shaped Sibley tents occupied the expanse of ground between the fort's buildings and the town, temporary quarters for the soldiers.

On the western bank of the winding creek, away from the post itself, a little town of shanties and tents had sprung up. Already music and laughter echoed from the doorways. When the wind picked up, the odor of homemade mescal drifted past. More than a few soldiers lounged around the little town, bragging loudly of their exploits during the war or seeking favors from the ladies.

It reminded Whit of Abilene when the cattle outfits hit town. There were shantytowns like that one straddling the outskirts of every army fort south of Laramie. He never knew a soldier to save a month's pay, not when whiskey and easy women were so close at hand.

Whit turned away from the creek and returned to town. There'd been days when he would have been down there with the soldiers, gambling and swearing and drinking with the best of them. Now, with the farm burned, his mama in her grave, Katie and Marty gone south, Whit had no heart left for such carefree ways. A terrible sadness seemed to swallow him.

When he reached the town square, Whit inhaled the wonderful aroma of fried chicken and sweet honey. He'd eaten nothing all day, and his stomach reminded him of the fact. The scent overpowered him, and he followed it like a trusted old bloodhound. He soon found himself at the door of the Stratton House, a small boarding establishment.

It had once been a hotel, the Excelsior. There were eight rooms upstairs, and a dining room, bathhouse, and kitchen below. Gingham curtains had replaced the fancy New Orleans drapes that helped give the Excelsior its reputation. But the old hotel featured a decent dinner, and the chicken promised to match Whit's mother's best efforts.

Whit kicked the dust off his boots and removed his hat before opening the door. He stepped cautiously inside, nodded to a pair of gentlemen speaking with midwestern accents, then continued on to the old front desk of the hotel. Soon a young woman in her late twenties stepped out of the kitchen.

Whit knew her at once, in spite of the years. She was wearing a white cotton apron over a yellow checked dress. She'd tied her amber hair up neatly in the back. When she spoke, Whit felt his legs wobble.

"Can we do something for you, sir?"

"Lucy?" he asked, fighting to catch his breath.

"Yes," she said, searching his face for something familiar. "Do I know you?"

Whit stared at the simple gold wedding band on her left hand and sighed. He considered leaving. The sparkle in her eyes brought back too many memories.

"You might," he finally whispered. "A long time ago you had a speckled pony named Henrietta. She had a rough time keeping shoes, and you used to complain it was the blacksmith's doing."

"It can't be," she gasped. She grabbed his shoulder as her legs threatened to give way. "Whit?"

"That's what I tell myself." He helped her to a nearby chair. "It's been a long time."

"We all heard you'd been killed. Have you seen Katie?"

"Just got here. I didn't know about . . ."

"I know," she said. She took his hand and held it tightly. "I get letters from Katie every month or so. She and Marty live in Waco now."

"So Ruben told me."

"I should have known. Oh, I almost forgot my

dinner. Whit, you will eat with us tonight, won't you? I could feed a regiment of cavalry here. Sometimes I do."

"It's why I came in," he said, and followed her into the kitchen. "Of course, I might not be respectable company."

Lucy smiled as he scratched his beard.

"Do you remember where the bath is?" she asked. "I recall scrubbing you once when you got yourself rolled around in the stable stalls."

"I remember," Whit said, trying to keep his face from turning pink.

"I'll send Billy in with towels and hot water. Do you have a change of clothes?"

"Afraid not," he admitted.

"You're thinner than Will, but a belt will take care of that. Hurry so you won't miss dinner."

"I wouldn't do that if I had to come naked."

"Watch yourself, Whit Macomb," she warned. "The marshal sometimes sits with us at supper."

Whit smiled as she swept the hair back from his forehead and planted a kiss there.

"It's good to see you, too," he said, touching her shoulder with a tenderness he'd thought lost years ago.

Before either of them could say anything more, Whit turned and walked toward the bathroom. It was a sobering thought, Lucy married. But it was only to be expected.

By the time Whit had shed his clothes, a small blond-haired boy of six or so walked in and poured a kettle of hot water into a wooden tub.

"I'll get some more water, mister," the boy said, disappearing as fast as he'd come.

Whit smiled, then emptied a bucket of cool

water into the tub. With his foot he helped the warm water circulate. Another kettle of hot would make it near perfect. There was a cake of soap nearby, and Whit took it with him to the tub. The boy appeared with the second kettle, and the bath was ready in no time.

"Mama said you should hurry," the boy whispered as Whit climbed into the tub.

"Is Lucy your mama?" Whit asked as he began scrubbing a week's dust and sweat from his hide.

"Yes, sir," the boy said as he gathered up Whit's discarded clothes. "Guess it's been a long time since you had a bath, huh?"

"Awhile," Whit admitted, laughing as the boy held the filthy clothes at arm's length.

"I never like baths much myself," the boy confessed. "But I never got away with skipping 'em for a whole year."

Whit laughed again. It felt good, laughing. And relieving himself of all that accumulated filth didn't hurt his spirits, either. When the boy returned, he brought clean clothes and a razor.

"These were my papa's," the boy announced. "Razor's sharp enough to split hairs."

"Thanks," Whit said. "Your mama said your name was Billy."

"William, really," the boy explained as he spread the clothes out on a small table beside the tub. "But nearly everybody calls me Billy."

"Mind if I do?"

"No," Billy said, smoothing out a wrinkle in the shirt.

"Tell your papa I thank him for the loan," Whit said, nodding toward the clothes.

"I can't," Billy mumbled.

"You can't?"

"He died just after Christmas, two years ago."

"I'm sorry," Whit said. He climbed out of the tub and wrapped a towel around his waist.

"You knew Mama before, huh?" Billy asked, gazing up into Whit's eyes.

"From when we were kids," Whit explained.

"She likes you a lot. Isn't everybody she'd loan Papa's razor."

"I like her, too," Whit said as he dried himself.

"You got a lot of scars," Billy said. He pointed to the jagged line which cut its way across Whit's shoulder.

"I've been off fighting Yanks and Indians, Billy. It takes its toll."

"Shhh," the boy whispered, coming closer. "We got a lot of Yanks here. Mama says you shouldn't call 'em that."

"I understand," Whit said, resting his hands on Billy's small shoulders a moment. "I guess your mama's had a rough time here."

"She's got Ben and me to help. Sometimes Julie Henderson hires on to clean and help cook."

"I see. Well, Billy, I suppose I'd better get myself shaved and dressed. I don't suppose people go to supper here naked."

"No," Billy laughed.

"Thanks for the hot water and the clothes."

"You're welcome."

As Whit lathered up the soap and spread it across his cheeks, Billy backed out of the room. Ten minutes later Whit Macomb appeared in the dining room, shaved and washed and sporting clean trousers and a freshly starched shirt.

"Gentlemen, I'd like to introduce an old friend,"

Lucy said as he walked to the table. "This is Whitman Macomb. His family pioneered Jack County."

The three men at the table stood and nodded to Whit. Billy smiled, and a slightly smaller boy huddled closer to Lucy.

"My boarders, Whit," she said, pointing to the men. "Judge Baker, who runs the courthouse. Mr. Carlisle and Mr. Atwood, who are partners in the mercantile."

Whit shook hands with the men, reading suspicion in each man's eyes.

"You've met Billy. This is Ben, my youngest," Lucy said. She hugged the smaller boy and whispered something in his ear.

"Nice to meet you, Ben," Whit said, smiling.

"Enough with all this business," Carlisle said. "Let's get back to important matters. Like dinner."

Everyone seemed to agree, and soon the chicken and biscuits were passing around the table in a flurry. Corn was being gnawed from the cob, and the scent of honey was everywhere.

After each diner had satisfied himself, Whit helped Lucy clear the table. The boys were dispatched to fill the kindling box, and the boarders retired to the front parlor for a friendly game of cards.

"Must be hard to run this place by yourself," Whit said as Lucy began washing the dishes.

"When did anyone around here ever have it easy?" she asked, smiling at him. "I never knew you to flinch from hard work, and you've had more than one lifetime's share of it."

"Tell me about your husband."

"It hurts to talk about it," Lucy told him.

"I want to know, Lucy. We never had any secrets, not the two of us."

"I know. But it's all something I've left behind me."

"Tell me. Please?"

"His name was Will Stratton. He bought the Excelsior just after you left. I would have waited for you, Whit. You know that. I even asked you to let me. We had word you were killed somewhere in Tennessee, and the life just about went out of me. Will helped me recover.

"I don't know that I really loved him. He was nice to me, and I had few other prospects, what with so many of the young men off fighting. I was a good wife to him, Whit."

"I never thought different."

"And all in all, it was a fair bargain. I got the two boys, this place free and clear."

"What became of him?"

"We wanted the hotel painted. That was before I turned it into a boardinghouse. More need for that in Jacksboro than a fancy hotel."

"Go on."

"He was up on a ladder, working well after dark. Coming down, he fell. It wasn't even far to the ground. But his head hit the ladder. Dr. Garfield said he died quickly, and we should be glad he wasn't paralyzed. It's hard to feel glad, left with a family to raise and no man around."

"I know. Mama went through that."

"She had you, though, sixteen and near a man."

"You seem to have a little help yourself," Whit said, pointing to the boys, who were dropping slivers of wood into the kindling box.

"I know." She continued with the dishes.

Whit picked up a linen towel and began drying the scrubbed plates.

"This brings back memories," Lucy said. "You used to help me with my chores so we could take a moonlight stroll along the banks of Lost Creek."

"Seems a fair enough bargain, even for old-timers like us."

"Is that an invitation?"

"I thought so."

"Then I accept," she said, pulling him over beside her. "Whit, I've missed you so much."

"No more than I've missed you," he told her as he slipped his left hand around her waist. They stood together for a moment or so, neither one daring to move for fear that the other would vanish. Finally they pulled apart and finished the dishes.

After the last spoon was put away and the boys safely tucked into their beds, Whit led the way out the back door toward the creek. The sky was clear, and a million stars seemed to be out that night. The moonlight showered them with a magical kind of glow, and Whit began feeling warm in a way that hadn't seemed possible the night before.

"What brought you back?" Lucy asked as they sat on a large boulder beside the creek.

"I don't know exactly," he replied, gazing at the stars overhead. "Papa's dreams, I guess. I wanted to build the farm, take care of Mama."

"And now?"

"Mama's dead, and Katie and Marty don't likely need me to help. Or to worry about, either. I guess Jack County's as good a place to build a future as anywhere else. The farm needs a lot of work, but I'm able. It won't be easy, but it's my home."

"Whit, there are things you should know."

"Such as?"

"Since '64 the Comanches have owned everything northwest of town. Anyone out there without a regiment of cavalry is in peril of losing his life."

"It won't be like that forever."

"There's more."

"What?"

"The new government collects taxes on these lands. Most of the farms were seized two summers ago for monies past due."

"You mean I don't own the land?"

"Exactly," she confirmed.

"So what do I do next, ride away and forget the price that's been paid for that ground? I've bled for it. Papa died there!"

"Oh, the land's up for public auction. Nobody's bought it. The truth is nobody wants it until the Comanches are contained. There's no way to make it pay. A man with five hundred dollars in gold could buy half the county. But who has the money?"

"I do," Whit said. He ground his teeth and stared hard at the creek.

"What?"

"I didn't spend all my time in the army, Lucy. I've been in the Dakotas mining, then later in Abilene, helping cattle buyers. I might not have five hundred dollars, but I've got close to that much, enough to buy back the farm and purchase some stock."

"Stock? Whit, the range is alive with stray cattle, wild hogs, and horses. If you could put an outfit together, you could round up a few hundred head in a matter of weeks."

"It's too late in the year to drive them to Kansas. The buyers will have left, and the grass is all eaten."

"Kansas? What's to keep you from marketing them right here in Jacksboro? The army needs beef at Fort Richardson," Lucy said. She pointed to the tents and makeshift buildings just south of the creek. "And there's Fort Griffin, out on the Clear Fork of the Brazos. The stage line buys horses. Whit, you wouldn't have problems selling stock, or getting it, either."

"It could be a real start, couldn't it?"

"You'd have to watch out for Comanches, though," Lucy warned. "They've been raiding steadily since the end of the war."

"I've fought Indians all my life," Whit said somberly.

"It would be a future, Whit, a good one."

"Like we used to talk about when we were kids. You still dream of that canopy bed and a two-story house?"

"With a vegetable garden and five kids scurrying around like little rabbits."

"It's been a long time since I've thought about that," Whit said as he rested his head on her shoulder.

"A long time," she whispered, sliding her arms down so that her fingers linked behind Whit's back.

"I've missed our walks together," he sighed. "Lucy, would it be disrespectful to call on you regularly?"

"I can't see how," she told him. "And I wouldn't have it any other way."

"You know, last night I thought I'd lost everything. My future, my dreams, my home. Now it seems like it's all been here waiting for me to turn over a stone and discover it."

"I know what you mean."

"I'll talk to the judge about the land tomorrow," he declared. "By next week I'll be building."

"We can make it work, Whit. I know we can."

"So do I."

It was well past midnight when they finally returned to the boardinghouse. By then every lamp in town had been extinguished. Whit slept long and soundly that night in the little room in Ruben's stable. A dozen dreams came to him, visions of Lucy and their future together. He would awake full of renewed hope and rekindled spirit.

Chapter Four

"I never knew Whit Macomb to sleep away half the morning," Ruben grumbled as he flung open the door of the little room in the back of the stable.

"Never had the chance before," Whit answered wearily. "I don't see it's any too light outside, either."

"Got my lantern burning. You need more light than that?"

"I can get around this stable blindfolded if I have to," Whit said, rising from his bed. "Now, what have you got in mind?"

"I wouldn't refuse an offer to help feed and water the horses," Ruben said, rubbing his hands together.

"You wouldn't?" Whit asked.

"No. And after all, a man usually does a little something to thank those who put a roof over his head."

"Well still in the forecourt?"

"It is, but I already set young Tom to fetching the water. Feed's in the corner like always."

"Then you go have yourself some breakfast, old man, and we'll tend to your chores."

"Old man?" Ruben asked, his eyebrows rising. "Me?"

"See anyone else around here with white hair?"

They shared a laugh. Then Ruben left, and Whit pulled on his clothes. After brushing back the long hair from his forehead, he continued to the stable and set to work meting out feed for the horses. Young Tom Morgan was filling the watering troughs. By the time the two had the animals tended, a cock announced the sun's appearance.

"He always have you up this early, Tom?" Whit asked.

"Oh, sometimes we don't go to bed at all," the boy replied. "Why, I recall about three weeks back . . ."

"I can see you've picked up Ruben's bad habits," Whit laughed. "I never met a man who could match Ruben for spinning tales."

"He does know a few," Tom agreed.

"Well, I've earned my keep for the day, Tom, so I think I'll see if Lucy might feed me some breakfast."

Whit slipped through the doors and made his

way through the misty morning to the Stratton House. He arrived at the kitchen door to find Lucy frying eggs.

"Need any help?" he asked through the door.

"Not with the cooking," she told him. "Of course, I'm always looking for a good dishwasher."

"That mean I'm hired?" he asked.

"Sure." She motioned him to join her at the stove. "But you don't have to wash dishes to get a little breakfast."

"I could pay for my meals."

"That's not what I meant," Lucy said, flipping her eggs. "I was just remembering the way you used to sneak into Mama's kitchen, begging for a biscuit or a slice of bacon. I swear I never knew anyone else who could talk her out of food day after day."

"I wasn't much bigger than Billy the first time." Whit smiled as he recalled it. But his smile soon faded. "That was a long time ago, though, and I gave up begging."

"You haven't changed as much as you think, Whit, as much as other things."

"I guess that's true," he admitted.

As Lucy finished cooking, she told Whit about his sister Katie and the two nieces he hadn't heard of.

"And Marty?" Whit asked.

"Works for Katie's husband, Ross Eckles. Ross has a dry-goods store. Marty hopes to read for the law soon."

"Marty a lawyer," Whit said as he snatched a piece of bacon and started chewing on one end. "It's hard to picture him even grown up."

"The farm could wait long enough for you to

visit them,'' Lucy said. ''The stage could have you there in two or three days.''

''No, there'll be time for that later,'' he said. He helped her carry the food into the dining room. ''There's the matter at hand first.''

''Which is?'' she asked as they returned to the kitchen.

''Buying back my home,'' Whit told her.

While Lucy fed Judge Baker and the other guests in the dining room, Whit sat in the kitchen with Billy and Ben, devouring bacon and eggs along with freshly baked rolls.

''Mama says you're going to raise horses,'' Billy said when they finally finished.

''Oh, horses mostly raise themselves,'' Whit explained. ''I plan to catch some, break them to saddle. We'll be rounding up cattle, too.''

''I like horses,'' Billy said. ''Mama doesn't let me ride, though. She says there are Indians outside of town just waiting to scalp me.''

Ben covered his head, and Whit laughed.

''Well, once things settle down a bit, maybe your mama will let me teach you how to ride,'' Whit said, touching both boys lightly on the head before leaving the table. ''We'll have to ask her.''

After the judge finished his breakfast, he drifted down the hall to the parlor. Whit followed, locating Judge Baker as Atwood and Carlisle joined in what promised to be a morning's card playing.

''Pardon me, Judge Baker,'' Whit said cautiously. ''I was hoping to discuss a business matter with you.''

''Well, Mr. Macomb, as you can see, I'm occupied at present.'' The judge indicated his fellow cardplayers. "I generally hear legal arguments in the afternoon."

"I've no arguments to make," Whit explained as the judge waved a halt to the game. "It's a matter of property."

"Ah, that would be the land along the Trinity between Lodge Creek and Jones Creek," Judge Baker said matter-of-factly. "You see, I do take my office seriously."

"Seriously enough to discuss a purchase price?" Whit asked.

"But never seriously enough to interfere with my morning," Judge Baker said, turning back to his companions.

The judge, Carlisle, and Atwood devoted themselves entirely to the game then, and Whit had to content himself with watching. The game itself seemed tame compared to the freewheeling contests Whit had witnessed in the Dakotas and later in Abilene. He'd played in such games, occasionally winning, more frequently escaping with his hide.

"You seem to understand the game, Mr. Macomb," Atwood said after the first hour. "Played before, have you?"

"From time to time," Whit confessed.

"Poker's really a game best played by four," the judge said then. "Care to take a hand?"

"Of course, we don't play on credit," Atwood said.

"I've got little better to do," Whit said, pulling out his pocketbook and removing fifty government greenbacks. "So I might as well."

"New money is always welcome," Carlisle said as he passed the cards to Whit. "New player always deals."

Whit took the cards, shuffled three times, and passed them back so Carlisle could cut the deck. Whit then dealt the four hands and studied his cards. Before long he'd lost himself in the game.

Whit often observed the other players taking long looks out of the corners of their eyes. He held his own cards close to his chest. The other players wagered seemingly by instinct, and Whit had a difficult time predicting them. For his part, he played Dakota style, rarely taking wild chances, betting heavily only when he held high cards.

"You play awful soft for a Texan," Judge Baker told Whit.

"But he stretches his dollars," Atwood pointed out.

Whit soon found himself seemingly playing against the combined skills of the three northerners. He often had difficulty reading the judge's eyes, though Atwood and Carlisle betrayed their strengths with flashing grins and their weaknesses with tapping fingers and nervous feet.

It's not so different from battling Sioux war parties, Whit thought as he played hand after hand. He had to read intentions, avoid the temptation to jump into ambushes, make a decision and stick to it.

"Mrs. Stratton mentioned you fought with the rebels," Atwood said when young Billy brought in glasses of mint tea.

"I served my state," Whit explained. "Most of the people here in Jack County voted against seceding, but once it was done, it was done."

"Your family paid a high price for your loyalty to the South," Judge Baker pointed out. "You lost your home, your livestock, the land itself."

"We've always paid a price, Judge," Whit said, fighting to keep the bitterness inside him from flowing into his words. "I suspect we'll pay it again. It's what makes us what we are."

"And what's that?" Carlisle asked.

"I'm not always certain," Whit admitted. "I've never found words for it. Maybe there are none. But inside, I know what it is, what it feels to be a Macomb, to control my destiny."

"It never fails to amaze me," the judge said. "You people. I understand there were a thousand people living in Jacksboro in 1860. Now there aren't half that many in the entire county. Two-thirds of the land is up for auction, only no one's willing to bid for it. You have no economy. If it wasn't for the fort, the town would blow away in the first good dust storm. If the Comanches didn't burn it first."

"Then why did you come here?" Whit asked the three men. "There have to be better markets for goods."

"We supply the whole county," Atwood explained. "We can buy cheap from the north and sell here at premium prices. There's little choice. If a man needs a rifle, he buys from us. If he needs a pair of shoes, where does he go?"

"We do all right," Carlisle added. "Not as well as when the cavalry runs down the Comanches, but we still make more than when we competed against three other places in Columbus."

"And you, Judge?" Whit asked.

"I had a federal appointment," Judge Baker explained.

"So you're paid a salary," Whit noted. "And?"

"I have a certain influence over contracts. Sometimes I help someone acquire a particular piece of land."

"What about my farm?" Whit asked. "How do I go about acquiring it?"

"First of all, have you signed your loyalty oath?" Judge Baker asked.

"Yes," Whit told them. "I earned it the hard way, too — serving in the federal army up in the Dakotas, along the Bozeman Trail."

"He's a galvanized Yankee," Atwood laughed. "And here we were worried he might cause trouble."

"Some returning soldiers have stirred up resentment against the local authorities," Judge Baker explained. "But as you said, here in Jack County people for the most part have welcomed us. There weren't many slaveholders here, I gather."

"Not many," Whit said. "I remember a couple of slaves being bought on the square, though. They had an auction. Mama wouldn't let me watch, and Reverend Henriks spoke up against it."

"So what you'll be out are the taxes, our levies, and next year's taxes paid in advance," the judge finally said. "It will take time to figure exactly, and I'll have to know the boundaries you want."

"I thought you said you were familiar with the property," Whit said.

"Ah, but you surely won't want the same exact place. For one thing, your old boundaries don't touch the Buffalo Springs road. The old Henry ranch and your place disputed some acreage, but I sold the eastern Henry range to a cousin, a certain Nelson Henry. You might want to extend your lands to Crooked Creek."

"That would mean a third more land," Whit said, digesting the idea.

"There are some filing fees, and the papers would have to be drawn, but in the end it would likely cost you six, maybe seven hundred dollars."

Whit frowned. The land his father had died for appeared to be priced less than a dollar per acre.

"That too much?" the judge asked.

"I'll raise the money," Whit said, counting his bills. He'd managed to collect seventy-two dollars just playing cards. But he knew such luck wouldn't continue.

"Well, are you going to stay here the rest of your life, Whit Macomb?" Lucy asked then, resting her hands on her hips. "I thought you offered to help wash the dishes."

"I did," Whit said and turned the cards over to Judge Baker. "Let me know when you come to a total, sir. I've got a little over five hundred dollars now, and I'll manage the rest soon."

"You've either been robbing banks or were uncommonly lucky at cards," Judge Baker said, wiping his forehead with a handkerchief.

"Just had lots of time to save it," Whit explained. "I'll be by the courthouse later."

"I'll look for you," the judge replied.

Whit then left with Lucy. But when they reached the kitchen, he discovered the dishes were done.

"I don't understand," Whit said. "Why . . ."

"I have to have those men here as boarders,"

Lucy told him, "but I don't have to sanction their games. I've seen poor farmers cleaned out."

"I won seventy-two dollars," Whit told her. "And I think the judge will allow me to buy back the farm."

"Well, that at least is good news. I have more. Colonel Burnett finally started ordering more active cavalry patrols. One left at dawn. Maybe they'll drive off the Comanches."

"What do you know of this colonel?"

"Not much," Lucy confessed. "I've had him over sometimes on Sundays, but he keeps to himself. The younger officers talk my head off."

Whit was to have his own chance to appriase the work of the cavalry soon enough. After lunch he met Judge Baker in the old stone structure on the square that had once been a Masonic lodge, later a warehouse, then army headquarters, and finally a courthouse. Before Judge Baker had a chance to add any figures, Whit heard a loud commotion outside.

"Cavalry's back!" someone screamed.

"Oh, God, they've been attacked."

Whit didn't hesitate. He raced outside in time to glimpse a bedraggled assortment of blue-clad soldiers stumbling into town from the north. Some carried wounded comrades. Others held limp arms as they walked. Whit detected bandaged shoulders and heads among the group. Only one or two were still on horseback.

Colonel Burnett rode through the command, uttering curses and shouting commands. The colonel then turned toward the courthouse, dismounted, and charged up the steps to Judge Baker's office.

Whit stepped out of the way, then followed the officer back inside. The dusty column of soldiers continued to stream past, many dragging their carbines in the street. Aside from a few of the officers' mounts, only ten mules remained with the command.

"A disaster," Colonel Burnett declared. "From the very beginning. How can we be expected to pursue Indians on mules that should've been turned into shoe leather six months ago? Most of the regiment still carries those cumbersome rifled muskets. We need more carbines, and some of those new repeating rifles."

"We need many things, John," Judge Baker said. "I'll send a wire, but you know the budget is tight."

"Yes, I know," Colonel Burnett said, sighing.

"What you need are better tactics, a new style," Whit said, feeling a chill run down his spine as Colonel Burnett turned his way.

"Oh?" the colonel asked. "And just who are you to tell the U.S. Army how to fight Indians?"

"I'm Whit Macomb. I served with the Second Texas until Vicksburg, then rode with the cavalry. I've fought Sioux and Cheyenne up in the Powder River country, and Comanches since I was old enough to walk."

"You were a Reb then," a youthful-looking captain said, joining the discussion. "No other military training? The last one to give the colonel advice on the campaign studied Napoleon."

"None of these Comanches have studied Napoleon," Whit said, "but their tactics are superb. They keep their base mobile. Instead of a concentrated army, they rely on small attack groups, raising havoc everywhere. Quantrill kept you boys guessing till close to the end of the war. Who do you think taught him?"

"So, what would you suggest, Mr. . . ."

"Macomb," Whit told them. "Whit Macomb. First of all, you'll catch no one on an army mule."

"We've only got ten of those," the colonel said in disgust. "Most of our stock is gone."

"Comanches like mules," Whit said. "They eat them."

"We're practically horseless," the young captain said.

"Well, I know where I can find some horses if there was to be a market for them," Whit said.

"A hundred?" Colonel Burnett asked. "What price?"

"Ten dollars a head for mustangs," Whit said. "Twenty for anything better. That allows me enough to pay a crew."

"A bargain," Judge Baker said, smiling. "Tell you what, Macomb. I'll draw up a contract. You receive ten dollars a head for horses you deliver on the post suitable for riding. Ten more for the better mounts. But instead of paying you cash, I mark it off against your tax bill."

"How much is that?" Whit asked.

"Eight hundred seventy dollars for the land," Judge Baker said, scratching his head. "Of course there'll be a dollar-a-head tax on the horses."

"What?" Whit asked.

"We have to tax all cash assets, and that includes stock," the judge explained. "We'll be happy to take a hundred animals."

"That'll leave me thirty dollars to pay my men," Whit said. "Assuming we bring in a hundred horses. I'll have to offer them more, at least a dollar a head."

"You work that out for yourself," Judge Baker said. "We'll expect the animals to be turned over to Colonel Burnett by the first of September."

Whit nearly fainted when the judge mentioned such an impossible deadline, but he later discovered there would be public bidding on all contracts awarded afterward.

So I guess I've got a lot of work to do, Whit told himself as he left. And few to help. But if I can do it, the farm's mine.

Chapter Five

No single man ever tracked down a hundred mustangs, much less got them broken to saddle. But as Whit approached old friends and one-time neighbors, he found but one response to his offer of work.

"I wouldn't take to the open range for ten dollars a day," one said.

"My hair's a lot more precious to me than a few Yankee greenbacks," another told Whit.

Whit Macomb was never a man to give up on a

dream, but an afternoon of failure did little to lift his hopes. He even sent a telegram to his brother Marty in Waco.

"Unable to come at present," was the five-word response.

"At present?" Whit grumbled as he made his way down the dusty street to Ruben's stable. "When? Can't he see there'll be no future if we don't act now?"

"Trouble is," Ruben said when Whit repeated his complaint, "you aren't asking the right people. You run around town talking to people scared to death of Comanches. Most are already working at something. You want to find men like yourself, who need the work and the money, who don't shy away from a tangle or two."

"You might be a little old for running down mustangs, Ruben," Whit told his old friend. "And you do keep a little busy around this place."

"You might take Tom, though."

"He's awful young, Ruben."

"Fourteen — about the age you were when I took you with me chasing buffalo."

"Any other suggestions?" Whit asked.

"You remember Ed Quinby and his younger brother Charlie?"

"I ought to. They were with me at Vicksburg."

"They've been trying to keep their place up on Cottonwood Creek going. You know Ed. Hates to ask for help, but I know he's barely hanging on. I buy a pony or two from him now and then. I'll bet that's the only cash he brings in."

"Thanks, Ruben," Whit said, shaking the old

man's hand. "I'll ride out and have a chat with them."

"Want me to ask Tom?"

"If you'd rather, I'll speak with him tonight myself. I'll be back for supper."

"I don't mind talking to the boy."

"Then tell him we'll meet where the Buffalo Springs road crosses the Trinity. And to be prepared to stay out there awhile."

"I'll tell him," Ruben promised.

After saddling his horse, Whit rode northward across the empty Jack County landscape. He discovered the Quinby brothers herding two dozen rangy longhorn cows down Cottonwood Creek. Ed, the older at twenty-six, was tall as ever, sandy blond, and soft-spoken. Charlie was an inch shorter, but otherwise looked the same, only a bit younger.

"Thought the Yanks had buried you for sure, Whit." Ed paused long enough to throw a glance Whit's way. "But I suppose any man that's kept his scalp in Comanche country's more than a match for bluecoats."

"Truth is, I was a bluecoat myself for a time. Got an offer for you, Ed." Whit took off his hat and wiped the sweat from his forehead.

"In the market for a few range cows?" Ed's younger brother Charlie asked.

"Actually, I need your help. I've got a contract to deliver a hundred horses to the soldiers at the fort."

"Fort Richardson?" Ed asked. "Can't be. Those Yanks don't buy local."

"This is more in the nature of a trade," Whit explained. "I deliver the horses, and I get my place back from the Yanks."

"You're paying the back taxes then," Ed said, nodding. "Might have been cheaper to buy the property at auction. We got our piece back for a hundred and fifty dollars."

"And you have to keep the taxes up from here on out," Whit said, eyeing the cattle.

"Not so easy, either," Ed admitted. "We sell a few animals sometimes. Half the time the Indians run them off as fast as we collect them. You told us why you want our help, Whit. Now give me a reason for pitching in."

"Don't have a real good reason for you, Ed, Charlie," Whit said. "All I can manage is a hundred dollars for the crew, and the work will be hard. But while we're together, we'll mostly be safe from attack, and if we deliver, there could be another contract later. That we'd split even."

"Who've you got lined up, Whit?" Charlie asked.

"Nobody for certain. Young Tom Morgan who helps Ruben at the stable."

"He's a boy," Charlie grumbled.

"You weren't much older when you marched with us to Corinth," Whit reminded Charlie. "He seems to know stock. I trust Ruben Gaines to know when a youngster's ready to do a job."

"So that makes four of us," Ed said. "That it?"

"You know anyone crazy enough to join up?" Whit asked.

"Nobody," Charlie said. "Most folks think we're touched just to ride this range."

"Could be they're right," Ed said. "A hundred horses, huh? Whit, I've known you to bite off quite a bit in your time, but never anything like this. We deliver them all together or as we bring them in?"

"Normally I'd say in one bunch, but with the Comanches out and about, I'd imagine we'd be better off taking them to the fort as they're broken," Whit said.

"I agree," Ed said, nodding.

"To the plan or to coming along?" Whit asked.

"Both," Ed said, turning to his brother. Charlie nodded.

"Then I'll meet you where the Buffalo Springs road crosses the Trinity tomorrow morning," Whit said, turning the chestnut stallion southward. "Agreed?"

"Agreed," the Quinbys replied.

Whit returned to Jacksboro late. Lucy saved him a pork chop and some corn bread from dinner, and he ate the food silently in the kitchen while Billy and Ben helped their mother with the dishes.

"Ruben says you're heading out to the farm tomorrow," Lucy said as she scrubbed the plates.

"That's right," Whit told her. "We've got a contract to deliver horses to the fort. I'll be able to buy back the place."

"I have an old wagon out back I never use," she said. "You could take it to carry supplies."

"Supplies?"

"You'll need rope, don't you think? Tools. There aren't any at the farm. Flour, sugar, coffee, anything else you choose."

"I guess I haven't planned this out so well,"

Whit admitted. "Can you think of something else I've forgotten?"

"I spoke to Mr. Atwood about a case of Winchester rifles he just received," Lucy said. "They fire fifteen shots from a magazine."

"How much does he want per gun?"

"Probably everything he can get," she said, laughing. "But you could probably talk him into selling them for a reasonable price. Not the entire case, of course, but six maybe."

"There aren't that many of us, and I already own a Henry."

"You'll need them before you finish out there," Lucy insisted. "Buy them now, before you have a lot of money. Later Atwood will want a hundred dollars a rifle. Trust me. I do a lot of business at that mercantile."

"Did you already place the order?"

"Yes," she confessed. "It will be loaded and waiting for you tomorrow morning."

Whit didn't know whether to thank her or resent the fact that she'd dabbled in his business. In the end he only kissed her good night and went to bed.

Morning found Whit leading the way north up the Buffalo Springs road. Tom Morgan followed in the wagon, spreading a blanket of dust out behind them a quarter of a mile or so.

"Just wanted to make sure the Comanches saw us coming, did you?" Ed Quinby asked when Whit arrived at the rendezvous spot. "I hope you said a good prayer for us."

"We needed the supplies," Whit explained. "Especially these."

Whit handed each of the Quinbys a shiny new rifle, then explained how to load the magazine.

"I heard these Henrys jam the third or fourth shot, and you're standing out there all alone," Charlie grumbled. "Give me an old Sharps carbine every time."

"I carried a Henry down from the Dakotas," Whit said. "I had some trouble with it, but these are Winchesters. They fire fifteen rounds without reloading, and the action is smooth, no hitches I can spot. Longer barrel gives it range and accuracy."

"That could be helpful if the Comanches pay us a visit," Charlie said, scanning the far horizon.

"So what's the plan for today, Whit?" Ed asked. "Young Tom going to hunt mustangs from that wagon?"

"He's got his horse tied in back. We'll make a camp at Hadley's Spring, then scout the horses. I need to cut myself some rope, and we can build a corral of sorts by roping off that little box canyon between the spring and Lodge Creek," Whit explained.

It took the remainder of the morning to drive the wagon along the south bank of the Trinity to Hadley's Spring. Another hour was devoted to constructing a rope fence across the mouth of the canyon. Finally the four horsemen mounted up and began patrolling the range.

By late afternoon they'd passed dozens of wild longhorns, and what seemed to be an army of wild hogs. But no horses.

"Don't forget," Ed said, shaking his head.

"There used to be a dozen farms up here. What stock the Comanches didn't shoot or steal took to the open range. You even spot a few chickens out here sometimes."

"They'd be tough to rope, though," Whit said, laughing.

"Truth is, there's been a lot of uncivilizing in Jack County," young Tom said, rolling his eyes around the way Ruben always did when something unusual attracted his attention.

"To tell you the truth, I'm glad the pigs are out here," Whit said. "I get tired of beef sometimes. Roast ham wouldn't make a bad dinner."

"No, it wouldn't," Charlie agreed.

They then set out on a wild pig hunt, charging down arroyos and up hillsides, turning the big porkers out of their hiding places and out into the open. Once a pig was surrounded, a Winchester barked and the animal became a candidate for the spit.

Nightfall found Whit and his three companions sitting beside a fire at Hadley's Spring, listening to the crickets chirping away and a wolf howling from the distant hillside. Whit grew nervous each time the howling resumed. He couldn't forget the face of that Comanche, the one with the black hand painted on his horse.

As Tom tended the pork, a new sound came to Whit's ears, the sounds of a foot snapping a twig not fifteen feet away.

"Shhh," Whit whispered, drawing his knife and waving the Quinbys to keep their guns handy.

Whit wove his way through the brush, keeping his eyes alert for some sign of the intruder. After turning a slow circle from the spring to Lodge Creek, he finally spotted a pair of slight-shouldered figures leading horses through the buffalo grass.

"Best stop right there," Whit said, fixing the unwelcome guests in his sights. "Who are you?"

"Would you be Mr. Macomb? Whit Macomb?"

Whit stepped out from behind a locust tree and examined the intruders. The first was a hand over four feet tall, his face filled with a toothy grin and long scraggly hair the color of an August cornstalk. The second was taller, but neither appeared to be any older than Tom Morgan.

"Who are you?" Whit asked, lowering the gun barrel.

"I'm Coley Adams," The smaller one spoke. "Tom said you were coming out after horses. Thought you might need some help."

"Oh?" Whit asked. "I didn't know you were thinking at all. I could be a Comanche, you know. All that yellow hair would look mighty nice on my lodgepole."

"We heard you earlier," the taller boy said. "Smelled the cooking, too. Coley, well, he's not much of a trail cook."

"And which one are you?" Whit asked.

"Oh, I'm Christopher McDermott," the boy said, extending a hand which Whit ignored. "Call me Chris. My brother Scotty fought in your company during the war. Got killed at Corinth."

Whit nodded sadly as he searched the boy's face for traces of the brother. Yes, the fair skin, the freckles, the strawberry hair all fit.

"We're friends of Tom Morgan," Coley said,

growing nervous. He kicked the dust from his boots and took off his hat.

"We'd work cheap, Mr. Macomb," Chris said. "Hasn't been much cash at our place since Papa died. I thought maybe you could pay us something maybe. If we worked out, I mean. If we didn't, you could always send us packing."

"How old are you, Chris?" Whit asked, scratching his ear. "I only remember Scotty having sisters."

"Five of them," Chris said, sighing. "But there's me, too, plus little Andy back home."

"And how old?" Whit asked a second time.

"Mary's the oldest. She's . . ."

"You," Whit said, resting a heavy hand on the boy's shoulder.

"Fifteen last month," Chris declared.

"I'm fourteen," little Coley said proudly.

"Boys, I can't take you out here with us," Whit said. "It's dangerous. I couldn't look your mamas in the face if something happened. You may be as old as Tom, but he's different."

"Because he's worked in a stable?" Chris asked. His hands shook as he looked Whit dead in the eye. "I've worked horses and cows all my life, Mr. Macomb. I'm steady. Ask Mama. I told her I was coming. She didn't say anything, but I know she'd be real glad to have some cash. I know there are Comanches out here, but it beats starving."

"You got a brother," Coley said then, his eyes growing red. "Could you stay home watching him get so thin he was sure to die?"

"Probably not," Whit said. "But won't your folks miss your help at home?"

"I think they'll be glad there's one less mouth to feed," Tom Morgan spoke from behind Whit. "I'm sorry, Whit. I told them you could likely use the help. Coley's a little small, I know, but Chris throws a rope with the best. Coley can ride anything with more than two legs, and he's not bad company when times grow hard."

Whit turned and read the plea in young Tom Morgan's eyes. It was hard to imagine Ruben's scrawny stable boy calling anyone small, though in truth Tom did have a few inches on Coley Adams.

"Can we at least stay to supper?" Chris asked.

"Can't turn a man away from dinner and call myself a Texan," Whit said, waving the three of them toward the campfire. But as they walked, Whit dreaded hearing what the Quinbys would say.

Chapter Six

Whit wasn't sure how it happened, but by the time the laughter had died down, supper was eaten, and the fire was doused, little Coley Adams and Chris McDermott were part of the outfit. Maybe it was the way the boys fired their own verbal attacks right back at their elder tormentors. Or maybe it was the feeling of family brought by having the youngsters around. Whit didn't know. But when the sun rained down on them the following morning and he finally got a good look at how Coley's ribs protruded, at his sunken chest, at the boys' thin arms and legs, Whit did know he'd never have the heart to send them home.

That morning as he handed Chris and Coley the last of the Winchesters, Whit felt his chest swell with pride. The boys listened carefully as Ed explained the loading and firing. And afterward not a word was spoken about their being too young or too small to pull their share of the load.

"I don't know how many horses we'll find out here," Ed told Whit as they prepared to leave, "but when those boys head back to town, I expect them to take a couple of cows back so there's milk and butter."

Whit nodded his agreement.

"Reminds me of those little ones back in Vicksburg," Charlie added. "Catching rats to eat. Walking skeletons, some of them."

"We brought it on them," Whit said sadly. "First with the war, and now with this peace."

"How so?" Ed asked.

"Because we've left the fields unplanted, the stock untended," Whit said bitterly. "Because after five long years we still haven't won the range back from the Comanches."

"You've seen starving Indians, too, Whit Macomb," Ed reminded him. "You told me about that ride north to the Red River."

"Yes," Whit admitted. "My heart went out to those people. But sooner or later they've got to find another way to live. Burning fields and houses is no way to grow."

"Sure," Ed agreed. "Once the Yank cavalry makes its mind up to go after the bands around here, it'll be over. I don't suppose there's been more than forty or fifty men around here since the Elm Creek raid back in '64. Mostly it's a few old bucks and the young ones out to prove themselves."

"Maybe," Charlie said, riding past them all out toward the Trinity. "But whoever's still here put a mighty big hole in the bluecoats the other day."

The six horsemen crossed the river at Comanche Crossing, carefully mixing their trail with the host of other tracks that disturbed the soft sand of the river bottom. Once across the river, Whit led the way westward through the gullies and creek bottoms that made up the northen half of the Macomb farm.

For two or three miles the land was covered with cattle and pigs, even chickens here and there. But there wasn't a trace of a horse other than the ones Whit's party rode.

"This used to be fair mustang country," Whit grumbled. "I can't understand not seeing at least one."

"Look there," Ed said, pointing to a path cut through the buffalo grass of the prairie. Pony tracks, lots of them, formed a trail toward Turkey Creek.

"Comanches," Whit whispered, searching the distant horizon. "Gathering their horse herd. Well, that explains lots of things."

"Like what happened to the bluecoats," Ed added. "Ran into roundup time."

"Gathering the herd before setting off to their winter camps," Whit said. "Got to move the lodges, the women and children."

"You know where they're going," Ed said, following Whit's gaze.

"Turkey Creek," Whit announced. "They'll have a camp there for the men, a dozen or so, maybe more, guarding the horses. Soon they'll be headed west into the buffalo valleys."

"You're not considering going after them?" Charlie asked, wide-eyed. "That's crazy, Whit. The three of us against ten, twenty, maybe thirty Comanches?"

"We'll catch them by surprise," Whit explained. "There isn't any other way to get a hundred horses, not if they've been rounding up every ranch horse and mustang in the county. Those Indians will have more horses than they can handle, and they won't be able to follow, not without risking the rest of their stock. We'll herd what we can right into Jacksboro, right into the arms of those soldiers."

"It could work," Ed said to his brother.

"It's crazy!" Charlie declared. "I still got need for my scalp, not to mention what's under it."

"I'm for giving it a try," Tom said, and the other boys gave a whoop.

"Shhh," Whit said, silencing them. "Either way, you boys are staying out of it. This is no time to break in a new hand."

"A Comanche my age would be going," Tom objected.

"This isn't like rounding up cattle or roping a mustang, boys," Ed explained. "It's no game. They'll be shooting at you. Anyone hurt will have to be left. A raid like this, well . . . it's hit and run. Run, run, and run faster."

"I can ride faster'n anybody, I'll bet," Coley said. "How many horses can you three cut from a herd? Shoot, my family's been stealing Comanche horses for twenty years. Comanches steal them right back. Then it's our turn again."

"He's right," Tom said. "You'll need all six of us."

"Ed?" Whit asked, turning to his old friend for support.

"They're here, Whit," Ed said. "Might as well be with us. There's a chance the Comanches might run them down anyway."

Whit shrugged his shoulders and sighed as he gazed into the eager faces of the boys.

"Only a fool looks forward to this," Charlie said.

"Yeah," Ed agreed. "But I don't suppose we were much different than that ourselves, charging up that hill at Shiloh, getting our company shot half to tarnation. Boys are half fool and half skunk, Mama used to say. I suppose she was right."

"It wouldn't hurt you to have a bath, either," Coley said, holding his nose.

"Enough of that," Whit told them. "We've got some serious planning to do."

Whit hid his companions in a ravine a quarter mile from where he suspected the Comanches had made their camp on the banks of Turkey Creek. He left his horse with Tom, then set forth alone on foot to scout the Indian camp. It wasn't hard to locate the horse herd. The smell alone was enough to attract notice. The Comanches had the horses herded between the creek and a high ridge fifty yards to the west. Boys stood watch atop the crest of the ridge, but no one watched along the creek.

Whit spotted a pair of campfires between a grove of hickory trees. Three or four Comanches busied themselves preparing dinner. Across the creek three or four riders nudged strays back into the herd.

When Whit returned to his companions, he drew a picture of the camp in the sandy ground.

"There are three, maybe four hundred ponies. Lots are government horses and mules. On the ridge are ten or fifteen boys. None are mounted. The men are in the camp. If we come around from the north and start the herd in motion, the horses will ride right over the Comanches. The whole camp will scatter, and we'll be able to run the stock right to the crossing and on to Jacksboro."

"Sounds easy enough," Ed said.

"Well, it's tricky," Whit admitted. "All it takes is for one of us to be spotted. Or shot. The thing to do, boys, is ride hard. Yell and shout to high heaven once we start. But no matter what happens, don't stop. The Comanches will swoop down on you like a hawk and pluck out your gizzard."

A sick look came over Coley's face, and Whit laughed.

"There are twenty of them down there," Whit continued. "But with your rifle, you're the same as five men. Moreover, you know what's happening, at least at first. They won't catch on till it's too late."

"You hope," Ed said.

"I sure do," Whit said, smiling as he read the fear in the boys' eyes. "You sure you want to go?"

Charlie glanced off across the prairie, and Coley trembled slightly. Tom nodded confidently, and Chris followed suit.

"I take that for a yes," Whit said. "Now, what I want to do is pair off."

"I'll take the runt," Ed said, grabbing Coley by the shoulders and lifting the boy skyward. "I'm used to little brothers."

"Scotty McDermott and I got our first tanning together," Charlie said, motioning to Chris. "Guess I can ride with another McDermott."

"I'm with you," Tom told Whit.

It seems fitting, Whit thought as he laid out the balance of his plan. Two prairie orphans and all.

As night settled in all around them, Whit set out with Tom for the western edge of the herd. Coley and Ed circled around, coming in from the north. Charlie and young Chris would charge down the creek, fire their rifles, and start a panic. If anyone was detected, it would probably be Whit himself, riding close to the ridge and its eagle-eyed guards.

There are always risks to any plan, Whit told himself as he and Tom rode along. But the guards ought to be concentrating on the western horizon, not looking for someone directly below. Maybe they'd grown lazy fighting soldiers who came in columns of twos, blaring bugles and sounding like a steam engine. Whit hoped this one night these Comanches would relax their guard just enough to allow a couple of hundred horses to be swept away.

Whit finally halted his horse only a few feet from the first of the horses. It wasn't possible to see his companions. Whit hoped to give them a minute or so before continuing. The animals seemed to grow more restless each minute. It was as if they sensed something was in the air. Tom nervously rubbed his hands together. Finally Whit waved Tom to follow and headed into the herd itself.

"Whaa-ohhh!" someone screamed from a hundred yards away. "Whaa-ohhh!"

Shots followed, and the horses stirred into motion.

"Now!" Whit yelled, and Tom fired his rifle.

"Yahh-hohh!" Whit yelled, slapping his leg and driving the animals forward along the creekbed. "Yahh-hohh!"

Other shouts filled the air. Startled Comanches cursed and dove out of the way. Boys whined as they scurried up the trunks of hickory trees to avoid the trampling feet of the ponies. Panic set in. Rifles fired in a dozen directions. Shouts filled the air. Through the middle of the creek rode a single warrior, his arm holding high a bright yellow shield marked with a black hand.

"Black Hand," Whit mumbled, waving Tom along at the head of the horses. Whit himself hung back, watched Black Hand cut off a dozen animals from the stampede, then head after more.

There was something unearthly about that Indian. Nothing, not the shooting or the shouting or the terrified cries of his injured comrades, seemed to affect him. It was impossible to see anything clearly in the dust and darkness, but even so Whit felt the eyes of that Indian, the bitter hatred burning like fire through the confusion.

"Ahhh-ayyy-wha-cotayy!" Black Hand seemed to be screaming. Whit recognized the fury in the words, though he had no idea of their meaning. In those words rested the same pain, the same anguish that always filled a man who had lost something dear to him.

"These are my horses," the words seemed to declare. "This is my land! You have no right to take it from me!"

Yes, we're alike, Black Hand, Whit thought as he saw Coley and Ed ride past at the rear of the herd. Yes, I know how you feel. It's not so different from any war, though. Soldiers may be alike, but only one side can win, only one of us can call this place our own. And one of us must leave . . . or die.

Chapter Seven

An hour before midnight Whit led the way into Jacksboro. The sound of two hundred horses, not to mention the accompanying cloud of dust, stirred the town into life. Dogs yapped from porches. Candles and oil lamps were lit. Yawning men and women staggered out of their homes, demanding to know the reason for such a commotion.

From the shantytown on the far side of Lost Creek came a stream of startled, half-sober soldiers, jolted out of their boredom by the sudden arrival of the horses. Behind them stumbled assorted dance girls and whiskey vendors, wash women and barflies.

"I do believe we've brought a circus to town," Ed said, scratching his chin. "What are we going to do with all these animals?"

"Let's head on down to the fort," Whit suggested. "Maybe we can rig some sort of corral for the night."

"The colonel might agree to that, especially as some of these are his mounts."

"Yes," Whit agreed, thinking to himself that if his luck held, another hundred would get the army brand before long.

With the help of the duty officer at Fort Richardson, a makeshift corral was erected by stringing ropes between trees. It wasn't possible to count the horses that night, and more than a few made their escape to the open range before Whit's wranglers could coax the last of the animals inside the corral.

"Colonel Burnett will want an account of your activities," the young lieutenant who'd helped with the corral told Whit. "I'll rouse him."

"No, let him get his rest," Whit said. "I'm tired myself. We'll talk in the morning."

"Where will we find you?"

"At Ruben Gaines's stable for the present. But I'll be over in the morning. You're holding a sizable investment for me."

When Whit rejoined his companions, he found Coley and Chris eager to ride home and tell their families of the adventure. Ed and Charlie were eyeing the lights across the creek. Tom proposed bunking at the stable.

"I'm bushed myself," Whit said, gazing at the few lights still burning in Jacksboro. "You boys have your fun," he told Ed and Charlie. "See you're in shape to work by noon, though. All of you," Whit added, turning to the youngsters.

He put his hand on Tom Morgan's shoulder and led the lad to where their horses were tied.

"We had ourselves a run tonight, didn't we?" Tom said as they untied their horses from a post oak branch.

"Fortune smiled on us this time, yes, sir," Whit replied. "We made old Black Hand mighty angry, though. I hope he doesn't catch me in the open anytime soon. Comanches know how to make an entertainment out of a white man's dying."

"Yes," Tom said sadly. "They cut up my whole family."

"Well, they'll have their work cut out catching up to us," Whit said as he mounted his horse. "Especially now that I've got their horses."

They rode the mile to the stable in no time, climbed down from the saddle, and put away their animals. Whit led the way to the little room in back, then kicked off his boots and dove into bed. Tom spread out blankets beside the door and crawled between them.

"Thanks for asking me along, Whit," Tom said softly.

"You earned your way today," Whit replied. "You'll be welcome along anytime you choose to come."

"Not everybody'd give a boy with no family the chance."

"You've got family," Whit declared. "Old Ruben. Shoot, he's been a father to me, too. Guess that makes us brothers of a fashion."

"Guess it does," Tom said, sitting up momentarily. "Feels good to belong somewhere."

"Yes, it does," Whit agreed. "Now get along to sleep. The long days begin tomorrow."

Whit slept through half the morning and would have dozed longer had not Ruben finally banged on the door.

"Must be those days spent as a bluecoat," the old man grumbled. "Sleeping till noon. Next thing you know he'll buy himself a top hat and a buggy."

Whit shared a laugh, then crawled out of bed.

"Lucy's saved you a slice of ham," Ruben said as Whit pulled a shirt on. "Best get shaved before meeting with the colonel. You know those Yanks. They like a man to look pretty before doing business with him."

Whit crossed the street and entered the Stratton House from the kitchen door. Lucy'd read his mind or, more likely, conspired with Ruben. She had the promised ham and a slice of toast ready. Two kettles of hot water sat atop the stove, and Billy had a tub ready.

"I found you a clean shirt and some trousers, Whit," she told him, "but you really ought to let me outfit you proper, now that you're a man of enterprise. Sally McDermott, Scotty's sister, does sewing."

"I generally just buy from the mercantile," Whit explained.

"With the prices they charge, you'll come out ahead letting me measure you and Sally do the sewing. The McDermotts can use the money, too. They've fallen on hard times."

"Young Chris rode with us," Whit told her.

"I heard. He's awfully young, don't you think?"

"Yes, but Scotty and I weren't much older the first time we were mustanging. You grow up fast on a horse."

A half hour later, as he sat soaking in the tub, Whit still couldn't get Lucy's reply out of his mind.

"Sure, they grow up fast," she'd said, nodding to little Billy. "Or not at all."

Colonel Burnett rode into town a little before noon. With him was a tall, stiff-backed Ohio captain, Louis Cloud. The two officers turned their horses over to Tom Morgan at the stable, then ambled over to the Stratton House and seated themselves in the empty parlor.

"Can I help you gentlemen?" Lucy asked.

"We understand there's a young horse thief hereabouts," the colonel said as Whit appeared. "We've got a little business to transact with him."

"That'd be me," Whit said, sliding around Lucy and extending his hand to the colonel. "I'm sorry we surprised your men at the fort last night, but I was afraid to keep the stock on the range with only six of us to guard them. Didn't want Black Hand grabbing those horses back."

"Black Hand?" Captain Cloud asked.

"Oh, I don't know that's his name, but I've got nothing better to call him. He paints a black hand on the rump of his horse. On his shield as well. He seems in control of the band we hit last night."

"If you'd sent someone to the fort, we might have grabbed the whole raiding party," Captain Cloud complained.

"Be that as it may, Captain, we might've lost the Comanches and the horses. Big troop like yours is sure to attract attention. I figured the horses were worth the gamble."

"And now Black Hand will be alerted. He'll be well beyond our reach," the captain said, shaking his head.

"He was beyond your reach anyway," Whit pointed out. "Turkey Creek's a good fifteen miles. Your men going to walk that far?"

"Enough of this," Colonel Burnett said, pointing toward the empty chair across the table. "Have a seat and let's discuss finances, Mr. Macomb."

"Sure," Whit said, pulling the chair out so the two men could see each other before sitting down.

"I don't see he's entitled to anything for stealing back horses that are clearly branded. . . ." Captain Cloud began.

"Excuse me," Whit said interrupting. "I know you may feel you're party to this since you lost those horses, but I can't deal with two men. One of you's wasting your time here."

The captain started to speak, but Colonel Burnett flashed a look of displeasure in Cloud's direction.

"You're quite correct, Mr. Macomb," the colonel spoke. "We are most grateful for having the horses back, and I'm certain we can come to terms."

"It was never in my mind to charge you for your own horses," Whit explained. "Out here, a neighbor brings in stray stock for his friends. That's how I look at it. There are a few other brands on some of the animals, too. I'd have them returned to the families that lost them."

"That's agreeable," Colonel Burnett said.

"As to the other hundred mounts we discussed, I'd like to get started picking out which ones you want. Some are probaby ready for saddling now. The others I'll undertake to break," Whit explained. "I'll work out the money with Judge Baker, if that's all right with you."

"More than fair," the colonel commented. "Now, tell me, Mr. Macomb, how did you reach Black Hand's camp unnoticed?"

"Oh, just used some old Reb cavalry tricks," Whit said, laughing. "We did a fair job of picking up new mounts from you bluecoats' depots in Tennessee. The trick is to do what the other fellow doesn't expect, I guess. And it's easier to slip a rider or two through undetected than a cavalry column."

"You wouldn't be interested in leading a scouting party after those Indians this afternoon, would you?" Colonel Burnett asked.

"I've got my crew to get organized," Whit explained. "Besides, by the time you got twenty men mounted, Black Hand would be clear to the Brazos."

"You overestimate this Indian," Captain Cloud objected.

"No, I don't," Whit said. "I've seen his type

before, on the Trinity and up in the Big Horn country. He smells trouble, sees in the dark. He turned your column upside down the other day, Colonel. No, you'd best get your men trained for hard riding and get to know this country better before going after this Black Hand. He's a snake that'll bite you sure."

After eating lunch at the Stratton House, Whit and the colonel rode to the rope corral. It took only an hour to cut out the sixty mules and horses bearing the distinctive USA brand. Another dozen horses belonging to the stage line or various townspeople were then delivered to their owners by Tom Morgan and his young friends. Of the remaining horses, some sixty were judged fit for riding. Sixty-six animals remained once the saddle-broken mounts were separated and turned over to the soldiers.

"Forty for you, Colonel," Whit said, "and the rest stay with me."

"Agreed," the colonel said, shaking Whit's hand. "Of the sixty we took, I count forty-six mustangs, fourteen of other breeds. I've marked it so on your receipt. Turn that over to the judge."

"That's my count, too," Ed announced.

"Thank you, sir," Whit said, a little surprised there'd been no haggling.

While Whit rode alone to the courthouse to settle accounts with Judge Baker, the rest of his crew herded the sixty-six horses out toward Hadley's Spring and the corral.

"I credit your account with seven hundred forty dollars," the judge said when Whit handed over the receipt. "Subtract sixty as tax on the animals.

That leaves six hundred eighty applied against your debt."

"I'll have the other forty animals in a couple of weeks," Whit said. "Couldn't we go ahead and draw up the papers? If need be, I'll pay the balance."

"Why don't we do this," the judge said, resting his boots on his desk and eyeing Whit shrewdly. "Once you deliver the balance of the contract, I'll owe you a balance of four hundred, minus forty as horse tax. That would leave you over a hundred dollars cash coming."

"I count it out a hundred and seventy," Whit said, feeling suddenly uneasy.

"Let me be honest with you, Macomb. We don't have any money to pay you. We don't collect many taxes, and we generally pay vouchers for livestock, food, and the like, which you hold for the arrival of the army paymaster."

"I don't suppose he appears very often."

"Supposed to come once a month. More often than not, it's twice a year."

"So what's your offer?"

"Your property, as I mentioned earlier, might be extended to bound on Crooked Creek."

"That slice you're talking about belongs to the Henry family."

"No, it belongs to the United States of America currently."

"I won't buy a man's property out from under him!" Whit declared angrily.

"No? It's up for auction. If you don't take it, someone will. It contains the Buffalo Springs road. The day will come when that's a valuable stretch. It also makes your place a better shape. If you feel strongly, sell it back to the Henrys later, if they're ever in the market for more acreage. It's a bargain price."

"I dislike the notion of taking advantage of hard times."

"You southerners," the judge said, shaking his head. "The war's been over five years! Men to the south have herded cattle to Kansas, made their fortunes. The people here sit around and wait for the Comanches to go away, for the cavalry to protect them. Macomb, you're the first one to really take a hand in what's happening. It won't take the others forever to catch on. You have to seize your opportunities. If I had the cash, I'd buy up the whole county. Someone will. This land will be worth a hundred times the purchase price in two or three years. Cattle are selling for twenty-five dollars a head in Abilene!"

"So why tell me?" Whit asked.

"Because you're the kind of man to hold off the Indians, bring stability up north. You'll make it possible for others to safely ranch the eastern and southern parts of the county."

"And who'd that be?" Whit asked. "Atwood and Carlisle?"

"They might invest some of their profits from the mercantile."

"And you'd be their partner, of course."

"Naturally," the judge said, smiling broadly.

"And the people who've lived and died fighting to hold their little farms would wind up with nothing."

"That's the reality, Macomb."

Whit never wanted to strike out at anyone so much as he wanted to hit that judge. But it would accomplish nothing. No, Judge Baker was right.

"I'll take the Crooked Creek sections," Whit sighed.

As he rode off to join the rest of his crew at Hadley's Spring, he made two quick decisions. The first was to pay Ed and Charlie immediately, let them pay off their land. The other was to see that the McDermotts and Adamses had clear titles as well, even if it meant dipping into his own pocket to pay the taxes.

"Remember what Papa always said," Whit said aloud as he neared the spring. "Take care of your own first."

But Whit couldn't help remembering something else — the way old Ruben had taken them in after the farm was burned, the days spent at the forge while Ruben patiently explained how iron could be worked and reworked.

No, Whit thought. There's more to it than tending your own business. Those who can have to look after those who can't. That was how Ruben had always put it.

"It's a good way to live your life," Whit whispered to the familiar rocks and hills. "And it's what I'll do."

Chapter Eight

Those next three weeks proved a busy time for Whit Macomb and his outfit. The last forty mustangs contracted to the army were delivered as promised, but not without long days of back-breaking work mixed with occasional Indian scares. Several times each day Whit found himself glancing over one shoulder, fully prepared for the sudden appearance of Black Hand leading a dozen young warriors. None of the men ventured far without a Winchester at his side, and a guard was posted each night.

As it happened, Black Hand and his band avoided Hadley's Spring. They turned up occasionally farther west, burning an occasional farmhouse or terrorizing a family or two. Captain Cloud mounted small patrols of the area, but the soldiers seemed to have little effect on Black Hand.

"A show of force is what's really needed," the captain told Whit more than once. "We ought to mount up the men and set off in four columns, scour the countryside until we trap those red devils."

Whit only smiled and shook his head sadly. It was easier to catch a mosquito in a butterfly net than run down Comanches on the open plains.

"Well," Ed was fond of saying, "at least they're keeping their horses exercised."

As the final weeks of September passed, Whit turned the last of the captive ponies over to Ruben Gaines for hiring at the stable or sale to the stage line.

"What now?" Tom Morgan asked as Whit handed the boy his twenty-dollar share of the wages.

"Well," Whit said as the others gathered around, "I don't know that there'll be much more market for horses. The Comanches will soon be heading for their winter quarters. But, of course, they didn't pay for their mounts anyway."

Coley laughed, but the others remained stone-faced.

"I can't pay a lot of wages now that our cash

crop is in," Whit explained, "but Lucy says there's a fair market for eggs, milk, and butter. The animals are out there. All we have to do is build a barn, a coop, maybe a house for us human animals."

"Charlie and I figured to pass the winter at our own place," Ed said, stuffing his bills in a shirt pocket. "But Jack County folks always help a neighbor put up a barn."

"We can help, Coley and me," Chris offered. "We wouldn't need a lot of cash, just a share in the take and meals maybe."

Coley nodded his agreement.

"Tom?" Whit asked.

"Well, I can't very well leave you out here on your own." Tom smiled. "I don't snore, and I smell better'n Ruben. That make me good enough company?"

"The best there is," Whit said, shaking Tom by the shoulders.

In truth, though, Whit had other company in mind, too. A farm wasn't really a home until there was a family around, a wife to add the gentle touches that rounded off the sharp edges, children to fill the cold emptiness of winter with the sounds of laughter.

For days Whit and young Tom Morgan rode the countryside, searching out the perfect spot for the new farmhouse. The old spot brought back too many memories, reminders of the past. Whit wanted something new, better, and not so close to Comanche Crossing.

Hadley's Spring offered rocky outcroppings,

fresh water, and good grazing, but it was far from town, neighbors, and help.

"There's a nice stand of willows over on Crooked Creek," Tom pointed out. "Creek winds around there so you'd have three sides closed off."

Whit nodded, and they rode over to inspect the site. It was the closest point on the property to Jacksboro, and not far from the Buffalo Springs road. But Crooked Creek ran deep only in the wettest months, and the ground there was subject to flooding.

On the other hand, there was a similar site near where Jones Creek emptied into the Trinity. Two hills crowned the surrounding countryside, forming a perfect spot for defense.

"This is it," Whit announced, envisioning the farmhouse, the outbuildings, barn, maybe even a bunkhouse.

The next morning Whit laid out the foundations of the buildings. He then contracted with Jacklin's Sawmill for lumber to be delivered. Within the week Ed and Charlie helped Whit frame the barn.

Each evening as Whit sat beside the rough timbers and gazed at the empty grasslands beyond, the terrible silence of the place pounded on his soul. He knew the isolation of the plains only too well. It was what had chased him across thousands of miles from the Dakotas through Kansas back to Texas.

"Seems like you're planning an awful big house for just two of us," Tom commented. A shy smile came to the boy's lips, and Whit matched it.

"You know I've got more than a farmhouse in

mind," Whit said, punching Tom's arm lightly.

"Ruben says you've had an eye for Lucy Stratton since the two of you ran bare bottom through the river."

"Ruben likes to talk."

"So, have you asked her?" Tom asked with a grin.

"Since when did you become an expert on such things?" Whit asked, pretending anger. "Boy like you spends his idle moments chasing coons through the hollows."

"I chase girls, too, now and then."

"Do you?" Whit asked, laughing loudly. "Well, I thought to speak to her once the house is built, once we get a steady income from the milk and eggs."

"I wouldn't wait as long as that," Tom said, shaking his head. "She's got Judge Baker and Mr. Atwood after her. You're not getting any younger, you know."

"Think I'm getting long of tooth, do you?"

"Man gets to putting a wedding off too long, he's apt to wind up like Ruben, talking to horses and taking in orphans. Me, I like horses as good as the next man, and I'm an orphan myself. Still, neither of them are fit for taking to a barn dance or lying beside on a winter's night."

"Girls are better for that, are they?"

"So my papa told me."

Whit looked the boy in the eye and broke out laughing.

"Truth is, you're right, Tom Morgan," Whit said, getting to his feet. "I'm not getting any younger, and Lucy might gallop off with the judge any minute now. Guess I'd best rush to town and ask her right away."

"Now you're talking!" Tom said, tossing his hat in the air. "Don't go and forget the flowers. You got to have flowers if you're asking a lady like Mrs. Stratton."

"Oh?" Whit asked. "And where am I going to find flowers in October?"

"I saw some thistle down by the road. It's not really a flower, but it's pretty."

Whit laughed at the idea, but as he rode toward town, he bent down and snatched a bit of the brightly colored thistle. His mother'd always been partial to it, and maybe Lucy would care for it, too.

He arrived at the kitchen door in time to help with the dinner dishes.

"What's that?" Lucy asked as Whit set the thistle aside.

"Oh, just something I picked up on the way. Thought it was pretty."

"Thistle," she said, admiring the deep blue color, then dropping the narrow stem in a small vase. "My mama was from Scotland, and she always told me thistle was good luck."

"I hope so," Whit told her, "because I'm liable to need some tonight."

"Playing cards with Judge Baker?"

"No, I'm bound on a far more dangerous mission," he said. "I'm out in search of a lifetime companion, someone to share my trials and tribulations."

"Been to see Ruben?" she asked.

"Wasn't Ruben I had in mind," he said,

swallowing. "Truth is, Lucy, I was thinking about going into the cattle business. Men down south have made regular fortunes driving cows to market. But a man gets to building a ranch, he . . . well, he needs to see some kind of future for himself. Riding all day, coaxing cows up the trail, well, that's no real life."

"It's not?"

"No, Lucy. What I mean to say is a man works hard, he doesn't do it so he can pass out his years singing to his horse around a campfire. I want a home, not a campfire."

"You're building one, I hear."

"A fair-sized place, too. There's a parlor, a kitchen, two bedrooms on one side, and room to add more on the other."

"Why would you add others?"

"Well, Lucy, you might want to have some more kids one of these days."

"What?"

"See, if we were to get ourselves married . . ."

"Married? You and me?" she asked, laughing.

"Well, we thought pretty seriously about it once," he said, placing his hands on his hips and looking her angrily in the eye. "It's not as far-fetched an idea as all that!"

"It's not?"

"I spoke to you about us keeping company, didn't I? We took our share of walks down Lost Creek. Don't you think it's time I stepped forward, made my proposal?"

"Oh, is that what you just did? I never heard a question, only an assumption."

"Eh?"

"A woman likes to hear that question, Whitman Macomb, even if she's heard it before."

"All right," he said, taking a deep breath. "Dear Lucy, will you do me the honor of becoming my wife?"

"Is that it?" she asked. "Will at least bent to one knee."

"Oh, Lucy, I'll ask you standing on my head if you want, only answer me," he pleaded, dropping to his knees. There was a high-pitched giggle from the doorway, and Whit detected Ben and Billy exchanging smiles at his expense.

"I guess they might as well come along in," Lucy said, leaving him kneeling as she ushered in the boys. "Billy, Ben, Mr. Macomb here's just asked me to be his wife. How would that suit you?"

"He'd be our new papa?" Ben asked, looking Whit over with suspicious eyes.

"Ah, he takes baths now," Billy said. "He doesn't spit tobacco juice at me like Mr. Atwood. It's all right by me."

"Ben?" Lucy asked.

Ben walked closer, poked Whit's stomach, examined Whit's boots, then stepped to one side.

"Well?" Billy asked, nudging his younger brother.

"He never gave me stick candy," Ben said, frowning.

"Who else'll you find who'll carry you on his shoulders?" Whit asked, lifting the boy up and setting him squarely atop those very shoulders. "What do you say, Ben? Think you could stand putting up with me?"

"I guess so," Ben agreed reluctantly.

"Now, Mrs. Stratton, what is your pleasure?" Whit asked, helping Ben back to the ground.

"Do I get to ride on your shoulders, too?" she asked.

"If you don't object to burying a second husband," he said. "Yes or no, good lady? Don't keep your suitor waiting."

"It's my right," she reminded him. "I don't know. The boys will likely turn into renegade Macombs, running naked through creeks, talking to horses, chasing wild Indians, and roping cows. Of course, it would give me the chance to finally grow that daughter I've been wanting."

"Sisters?" Ben and Billy asked, exchanging frowns.

"Could be a baby brother," Whit whispered.

"Then I wouldn't be the littlest," Ben said. "That'd be fine."

"Lucy?" Whit asked.

"I suppose I'm left with few choices. I wouldn't want a mutiny on my hands. Besides, you do spin a fair story, and you dry dishes fairly well, Whit. So, all things considered, I believe I'll agree to your proposition."

"Hoo-ray!" the boys shouted.

Whit laughed, then seriously took her hand and kissed it lightly.

"I'll speak with the reverend," he promised. "The house won't be ready for a time, but I'd like to have the wedding there."

"No, we'll have it here in the parlor," Lucy said. "It's too far for some of the folks to come to the farm."

"But we'll live there," he insisted.

"Once the house is finished, and I have a chance to hire a housekeeper and a cook to tend my guests."

"And the date?"

"Can you have the house finished in three weeks?"

"First week of November."

"I always thought to be wed on a Sunday," Lucy said.

"That suits me just fine," he told her. "I'll pass the word."

"And I'll see to the food and decorations."

"Good night, Mrs. Macomb-to-be," Whit said finally, giving her a farewell kiss.

"Good night," she echoed, hugging him tightly.

The boys stepped over to shake his hand, but Whit would have none of that. He picked Billy up in one arm, Ben in the other, and held them tightly. Their small arms felt their way around Whit's chest and responded warmly.

"Looks like I picked myself up a family, doesn't it?" Whit said, holding on to the children as he fought tears back from his eyes.

"I hope you're as glad of it when you stay up half the night with their coughing or have to pull them out of a nettle patch," Lucy said, smiling brightly.

"I will be," Whit said, easing them to the ground, "so long as you're at my side."

"I'll be there," she promised.

Chapter Nine

Whit became a whirlwind of energy those next few days. He and Tom brought two wagonloads of lumber from the sawmill at Cooper Hole. Bryce Jacklin arrived the next day with eight squared windows for the house, and glass panes were ordered from Fort Worth. Two stone fireplaces were built within the house to fend off the chill of winters along the Trinity.

With the help of Ed and Charlie Quinby, plank after plank was nailed into place so that the barn began to take shape. Tom rounded up half the county to work on the house.

"Almost anyone'll do almost anything right now for a Yankee dollar a day," Tom explained as his crew braced beams and nailed planks.

Ruben arrived to supervise the construction of two permanent corrals, offering Whit the chance to divert part of Jones Creek into a watering pond for the stock. With Tom's help, Whit also dug a shallow well to provide for the family's needs.

Cutting shingles for the roof proved the greatest trial. The newly cut post oak, which was perfect for beams and planks, hardened quickly so that cutting it was akin to banging on iron. Fortunately a stand of ash trees was located to the north, and the ash shingles proved equal to their task and far less brittle than the more familiar oak.

Once the roof was completed and the glass fitted into thc windows, Whit paid off the workers and prepared to apply the final touches that converted rough-hewn planks and oak timbers into a home for his soon-to-arrive family. Bunk beds were installed in the corner bedroom Billy and Ben would share with Tom. Winter forage for the livestock was gathered. Two dozen chickens were captured from the wild and placed in a coop.

When Ruben rode out in his wagon with his precious cargo of red paint, Whit discovered two small blond imps in back, dressed in ragged overalls and prepared to join in the work.

"Of course you boys'll have to leave the top parts for me and Tom," Ruben told the boys. "Don't believe your arms'll stretch that far."

There was something about paint and boys!

Whit couldn't help laughing as he watched Billy and Ben slap red onto themselves almost as much as on the walls of the house.

"I don't recall you were any different," Ruben said when Whit tried for the fourth time to convince the children to concentrate on the task at hand.

Lucy rode out in her buggy around noon, surprising them all with a lunch basket full of fried chicken and corn bread.

"This is going to be our home?" she asked as he took her through the house. "Couldn't you at least have put in a wooden floor? And all these windows! I'll never get the curtains ready."

"When it cools, I'll put the shutters up," Whit promised. "Just now I thought it needed the light."

"Needs more than that," Lucy told him. "There's hardly any furniture. I'll tend to that straightaway."

"It doesn't need curtains and furniture," Whit said, gripping her hand tightly. "It needs you."

"Well, the house may not need the furniture, but I do," she declared.

"I remember rebuilding the house after Papa was killed," Whit said. He sat with Lucy in the doorway where they could watch the boys paint. "We didn't have so much as a table to eat off of. Marty and Katie and I worked every night to put a chair or a table or a shelf together. There's nothing like building a house to give you the feeling of being home."

"I'm glad," she said. "For my sake, and for the boys'. They need someone tall to look up to."

"I'm glad of them, too," Whit said. "It doesn't make me feel like I've lost quite so many years. In time maybe they'll grow to trust me like their real father."

"It's happening already," Lucy told him.

"I've made my share of mistakes in this life, Lucy, but I did one thing right when I asked you to be my wife. It's funny, I suppose, but I never pictured anyone else holding down that job."

"I used to picture how it would be married to you, Whit, but things surely have turned out differently. I thought we'd be a pair of eighteen-year-olds, riding off to honeymoon in New Orleans or St. Louis. Things being as they are, we'll find ourselves spending our wedding night in the same house with three curious boys, listening to little feet running across the porch, voices whispering half the night."

"You're not sorry I asked Tom to stay on?"

"No, you're going to need his help with the animals. Ruben didn't say anything, but I know he hoped Tom would come to the farm. Jacksboro's no place for a young man just now. More saloons and pretty girls than a proper town has need of."

"Oh, a town can never have too many pretty faces," Whit objected.

"You!" Lucy said, hitting him across the head with her handbag.

The painting was completed the Thursday before the wedding, and Whit avoided town the two days that followed. Tom made a single trip each morning with eggs and milk, but the rest of the time the two orphans rode out collecting a few wild hogs for butchering while keeping a weather eye out for Indians.

"I guess our little raid taught them to stay clear," Tom said as they returned Saturday afternoon.

"No, they're out there," Whit said, pulling his horse around toward the river. "Come and see for yourself."

When they arrived at Comanche Crossing, Whit pointed to the fresh tracks made by a pair of ponies.

"Black Hand?" Tom asked.

"I'd imagine," Whit said, nodding. "Most of his men will have gone to prepare the winter camp, but not old Black Hand. He won't be far away. See, Tom, he knows what I know. Only one man can hold this land, and once any white man plants his roots, the Comanche's hour is over."

"Then he'll head westward?"

"Most would," Whit agreed. "But this one . . . well, he's different. He'll keep coming. Yes, I'd say we'll hear from him again."

But in spite of Whit's uneasiness about the Indians, he appeared that Sunday in new coat and necktie, washed and shaved, with hair trimmed by the barber at Fort Richardson. Colonel Burnett led Lucy down the aisle in lieu of her father, and old Ruben, wearing a necktie for the first time Whit could remember, stood at Whit's elbow as best man.

Reverend Henriks wasn't a believer in long

ceremonies. He read the vows, spoke a few words, and pronounced Whit and Lucy to be wedded.

The real excitement started as Billy and Ben appeared with long paper streamers and confetti. A room full of dignified citizens became a mob of screaming devils, throwing streamers and paper everywhere. Confetti showered the newlyweds.

"Can I kiss the bride now?" Whit asked in spite of the chaos.

"I would," the reverend said.

Whit then sealed the ceremony with a long, deliberate embrace. Immediately afterward he led the way outside, then escaped northward with Lucy from the paper onslaught.

When they arrived at the house, they found the place full of neatly wrapped packages and bundles of food. On the table was a brief note from Tom:

"Decided a wedding night ought to be peaceful, so the boys and I'll be up at Hadley's Spring. Good luck."

"You sure he's only fourteen?" Lucy asked as they sat together and began opening the packages.

"Could be he's growing up a little fast, even for a Jack County boy."

"Will they be all right out there?"

"Sure, Lucy. It's their wedding gift to us, I guess you'd say. I've waited a lifetime for this, being with you in our own house, sharing whatever comes with someone who'll understand."

"I know," she said, resting her head on his shoulder. "I feel that way, too."

Chapter Ten

Winter along the Trinity had never been the easiest of times. As November mists gave way to sudden downpours and furious winds, Whit prepared himself for the harsher months that would follow. They arrived soon enough.

Whit first felt a stiffness in his shoulder, a twinge in the bent fingers of his left hand. Gradually a sharper pain arrived, and his legs lost their usual power. His knees crackled, and his neck stiffened.

By nightfall the first blast of icy air crept through the plank sides of the cabin.

"We're in for it now," Tom said as he stacked additional logs on the fire. "Blue norther."

Whit nodded, drawing his little family together beside the fire a moment.

"Lucy," he said somberly, "you make sure the extra quilts are brought out. Tom, we'd best batten down the shutters and see the stock have feed."

Even as the first flakes of crystallike snow fluttered to the ground, Whit and Tom busily fastened the shutters. All eight secured, Whit pointed Tom to the woodpile, then headed for the barn. While Tom carried firewood inside the house, Whit saw that the horses and cows were safely put in their stalls. The water trough was filled and hay spread about. The chickens would have to rely on the protection afforded by their coops. Whit hoped the birds wouldn't freeze.

"These ones spent the last winter on the prairie," Tom reminded Whit. "They're not apt to give in to the cold."

Within the hour the norther had become a purebred Texas blizzard. Gusts of snow bombarded the house. Sheets of ice draped the trees, causing some of the branches to snap. By morning two of the great white oaks along the Trinity had exploded in a thousand pieces as the water in their hollow trunks expanded.

"I hope those coons that were living there got out," Ben sobbed, rubbing his eyes.

"What's this?" Tom asked, scooting over beside little Ben. "Coons have a way of knowing about storms, you know. Why, I'll bet they already found a better tree, don't you, Whit?''

"Think so, Papa?'' Ben asked.

"Never knew a coon not to outthink a snowstorm,'' Whit replied.

"See there?'' Tom asked pulling Billy over from the other side. "Trust old Tom to know coons and such. Now, how about a song?''

"That's a wonderful idea,'' Lucy said, clapping her hands. "You boys feel up to singing?''

"Sure,'' the little ones answered.

"Afterward we'll have some cocoa and a story from your father,'' she announced. "If you can talk him into it.''

"Please, Papa,'' Billy begged.

Whit gazed into the three young pairs of eyes and laughed. Sometimes Tom could be as little as the others. And other times . . . well, you'd swear the boy was forty.

"After the singing,'' Whit promised.

It was hard to keep track of the songs that followed. Only when Tom launched into a rather bawdy ballad about "Fair ol' Fanny'' did Lucy proclaim it was time for cocoa.

"Just when we were getting to the best one, too,'' Billy complained.

"I think that one's best left for the girls on the west bank of Lost Creek,'' Lucy said sternly.

"They already know it over there,'' Billy declared. "That's where we heard it first.''

Whit laughed so hard he nearly spilled the kettle of hot water in his lap.

"Maybe we didn't come out here quite soon enough,'' Lucy snorted.

"Can't keep boys from being boys," Whit told her.

The songs and the cocoa fended off the worst of the cold that evening. The terrible howl of the north wind and the crashing of the oaks outside made for a restless night. Whit discovered Ben and Billy curled on either side of Tom Morgan next morning, and Lucy, gazing at the scene, smiled.

"I don't believe you're the only one that's adopted those boys," she said.

"He's as in need of a family as I am," Whit explained. "I remember how it was with Marty and Katie after Papa died. We held each other a lot, even with Mama there. A family can be an anchor out here, can help you sink your roots in the ground."

"I know," she whispered. "How about fetching some eggs from the chicken coop?"

Whit nodded. When he opened the door, he was startled to discover a foot and a half of snow outside. The coop was half swallowed by the fine white powder. The chickens were all right, though. Once Whit sprinkled feed for them, those hiding appeared to grab their share.

By early afternoon the sun reappeared. Whit and Tom rode out to check the cattle up Jones Creek. Riding through the snowdrifts was nigh impossible, though, and they ended up trudging through the drifts on foot, every inch of them shivering from the cold and damp.

Locating the rugged longhorn cattle was no easy feat. The cattle had deserted the high ground. They clustered in gullies and creek bottoms, where some shelter could be found from the wind. They had managed to locate the bundles of grass Whit had left for them. Most of the feed was partially buried by snow or covered by a sheet of ice, but the midday sun tended to that.

The following day, just as the snow began to melt, the north wind howled and the storm returned. More snow and ice tormented the land. A few cattle actually froze, and Whit found a couple of wild hogs who had given way to the cold. Fresh bacon and steaks were welcome at the house, though. Whit was glad they hadn't had to chase one of those hogs through the icy hillsides.

The weather improved little through Christmas and into the first of the year. Two turkeys were shot for Christmas dinner, and Whit invited Ruben and the Quinbys for supper. A second celebration was held for Billy and Ben, their birthdays coming in January, with fine leather hats being the prize gifts.

January's close brought an end to four months of peace and prosperity. As Whit and Tom rode the range along Turkey Creek, they spotted a thin line of footprints in the shallow snow.

"Unshod ponies," Whit pointed out. "Six or seven, heavily laden."

Tom nodded his agreement, and the two of them became instantly alert. Whit was alarmed to find a war lance embedded in a blackjack oak not a mile from where Black Hand had made camp the night of the horse raid.

"See the cut feathers?" Whit indicated to Tom. "See the red markings on the lance?"

"I see," Tom said, his eyes reddening as he angrily knocked the lance from the tree. "I remember a lance like that lying beside my father. It's Comanche, all right."

"It's a warning, so to speak," Whit said. "They left it in plain sight so we were bound to find it."

"What does it mean?"

"Clear out. Get off my land before I have to chase you off."

"Nobody's chasing me anywhere," Tom declared, picking up the lance and flinging it into the center of Turkey Creek. "I came to stay."

"It's not just you and me we have to think of, though," Whit said, glancing over his shoulder in the direction of the house. "We'd best send word to Colonel Burnett."

They turned away from the creek and headed homeward. As Whit climbed the hill leading to the house, he discovered it wouldn't be necessary to send word to the army. A patrol of soldiers was watering its horses at the creek.

"Got some bad news for you, I'm afraid," Captain Cloud announced. "Comanches are on the prowl again. Burned out some people up north."

"Where up north?" Whit asked nervously.

"Cottonwood Creek. Quinbys."

"Tom?" Whit asked, glancing anxiously at his young friend.

"Are they all right?" Tom cried.

"Just did slip away," Captain Cloud explained. "Weren't but ten, twenty Indians. It's like those cowards to slip in and burn a house full of civilians."

"There's no such thing in this county," Whit declared. "Anyone old enough to hold a gun's been fighting for this land the last twenty years."

"Maybe I should go fetch them?" Tom questioned.

"Do that," Whit replied. "Till we can do better, they can bed in the barn."

"I'll tell them," Tom said, galloping off toward Cottonwood Creek.

"I don't know if that was the wisest of notions," Captain Cloud muttered. "What if he should run across those Indians?"

"We spotted their trail," Whit explained. "They're back across Turkey Creek by now. Left a lance in a tree down there — a warning for us."

"Warning?" the captain asked.

"Or a challenge. Means get out while you can," Whit explained. "It's winter now, and most of the Comanches will be off in their lodges. But come spring, you can expect the young ones to come riding."

"That may be." Captain Cloud glanced westward across Jones Creek. "But there won't be many who ride back. The Sixth will see to that!"

There was a cheer from the men, but Whit felt no surge of confidence. The Sixth Cavalry hadn't done much to deter Black Hand and a handful of companions from burning out the Quinbys. It didn't seem likely the captain would have any greater success against fifty or more armed Comanches bent on making themselves a name.

That night after dinner Whit sat beside the fireplace as usual, Lucy on his left, Tom and the boys huddled on the right. A hundred different thoughts raced through Whit's mind, but it was Tom who finally broke the silence.

"I was eight years old when they killed Papa," Tom began. "I'll never forget it. Who could? We were riding down south to buy supplies, just flour, sugar, and the like. Mama and Papa rode in front, my little sister Annie in between them. My brother Mike and I were in back with the goods. Mike was close to twelve, but nigh as skinny as a rail fence and short, like Coley Adams. We were singing, and I was strumming Mike's guitar. Then the Indians came."

"You had no warning?" Lucy asked.

"Oh, you remember how it was in '64. There were ten sightings a week out here. After a time, nobody paid much attention," Tom explained. "Papa tried to get to his musket. He'd traded the pistol in for the flour. But the Comanches were on us too quick. A big tall one ran his lance into Papa. Another one grabbed Annie and rode off with her. Mama got the wagon stopped, then tried to load that old musket. Another Comanche dragged her off, screaming to high heaven.

"Mike and I hid under a blanket. Those Indians went through our supplies, tossing flour all over the place, busting bottles and yelling. Then they tore off the blanket and found us."

"What happened then?" Billy pleaded, his seven-year-old eyes widening.

"Can't talk about it all," Tom said, backing away from the boys as his hands shook. "They took us over to some trees, tore off our clothes, then started talking about all sorts of things. I didn't understand a bit of it. One of them seemed to want to take us along with them, like Annie. But the tall one that lanced Papa hushed the others. He took his knife and . . . well, he killed Mike, cut me across the head and chest, left me for dead."

Tom unbuttoned his shirt and revealed a long, jagged scar that wove its way from under his left armpit down to his thigh.

"I closed my eyes and hoped I'd die," Tom continued. "I didn't, though. Next day old Ruben happened along with Ross Stewart. They gathered up Mama and Papa, wrapped Mike in a blanket. Then they looked around for Annie and me.

"I was off wandering around, bleeding all over the place, naked as the day I was born. Ruben took me in," Tom said, smiling for the first time.

"And your sister?" Lucy asked.

"Found her a couple of days later, scalped. Ruben said she must've cried too much," Tom said, wiping his eyes. "Comanches won't mess with a girl that young if she causes much trouble. Sometimes they take boys, but Ruben guessed it was a blood raid, out for revenge. They got it."

"I'm so sorry, Tom," Lucy said, rising and stepping to the boy's side. "It's terribly sad to lose your whole family in a single day like that."

"I told you so you'd understand why I'm going to stay here no matter what," Tom declared. "Whit, you saw that lance. These are the ones who killed my folks, scalped Annie, cut me and Mike. Even if you leave, I've got to say."

"Leave?" Lucy asked. "I don't understand."

"We spotted Comanche sign up by Turkey Creek," Whit told her. "Some of them came through and burned the Quinbys' place. Ed and Charlie are all right. Tom rode off to invite them to stay with us."

"They'll be here tomorrow," Tom said, still shaking.

"But Captain Cloud and his men are out there," Lucy said. "We'll be protected."

"He hasn't been able to protect his own horses," Whit said. "I wouldn't feel too safe because of him. No, from now on we'll keep our own guard. I don't want you or the boys wandering out of earshot of the house."

Ben and Billy nodded, but Lucy only frowned.

"I must have been crazy to turn my business over to Hannah McDermott and come out here," she finally said. "We're all of us at risk here."

"We have been right along," Whit said. "We survived the blizzard. We'll get through this, too. Ed and Charlie will be here, too, from now on. We've got a good position here on this hill."

"Besides," Tom pointed out, "Comanches don't really give warnings. They come. If they felt strong enough to attack, they would've."

Whit nodded, but he wasn't altogether sure the lance was just a bluff. There was something different about this Black Hand. He wasn't like other men. Why had he come alone that night to Hadley's Spring? Why hadn't he ridden in with a war party and shot Whitman Macomb dead?

I'm not like other men, either, Whit realized. I could've fired my rifle, too.

"What are you thinking about?" Lucy asked, breaking Whit out of his trance.

"Just how important you all are to me," Whit said, pulling the boys close and patting Tom on the shoulder. "Keeping you safe's the most important thing."

Lucy nodded her agreement.

But the real question Whit had to answer was how. Was there ever a way to really guarantee a person would be safe, anytime, anywhere?

Chapter Eleven

As the ground began to thaw, Whit grew more anxious for the safety of his new family. He rarely slept soundly, not even after Ed and Charlie Quinby moved into the barn. Comanche Crossing seemed quiet enough in the daytime, but each time Whit and Tom examined the sandy banks of the Trinity, they detected clear tracks of unshod ponies.

"I don't see how they can cut through here so close to us and not be seen," Tom would grumble. "They're not invisible!"

"Close to it," Whit declared. "They've learned to be a part of the land, just like the river and the trees. They belong. You don't notice a post oak unless you look for it. These Comanches are the same way."

"But I look for them," Tom objected.

"Later, when you've developed an eye for them, you'll be able to spot them. But right now you don't know what to look for any more than that Yank captain does."

Whit intimated the same thing the following week when Lucy invited Colonel Burnett and his officers to join in a night's entertainment at the farm. As the gentlemen gathered in the small parlor, singing old war songs and chatting about the dull duties of a frontier cavalry officer, Whit filled cups of warm rum and left Lucy to guide the conversation. She did her best to keep to lighter topics: the price of sugar, Texas springtime, the newest fashions out of New York and Philadelphia. But it was impossible to ignore the subject most on the men's minds.

"It's hard fighting these Comanches," Captain Cloud declared. "They don't stand up and face you. Instead they run away from the army, then sneak in like cowards to burn farms and murder women and children."

"They learn well," Whit told the captain. "I fought in the Dakotas with the army. We were the ones outnumbered for the most part, and we spent most of our time waging war on the Indian camps, burning the lodges, destroying the foodstuffs that would keep the women and children from starving come winter.

"It's the way we've dealt with the Comanche, too. Far back as I can remember the cavalry and the rangers sent armed parties deep into their country, destroying the permanent camps, ignoring the warriors. It's an effective tactic. Kill a man's family, and what's he got left to fight for? He gets reckless, careless, gets himself trapped and killed."

"But not this Black Hand," Captain Cloud barked, pacing back and forth. "He's a devil, I tell you. We'll discover two or three of his scouts out in the open. We'll take to chasing them, and he'll . . ."

"Have an ambush set for you," Whit said, interrupting. "Old tactic. Or else you'll ride down a road and find it blocked. While you're tangled in the brush, he'll hit the flanks of your column. He's been well schooled in tactics, no doubting that."

"Well, he'll soon meet his final reward," Captain Cloud boasted. "He can't be everywhere at once, and when we go after him this time, we'll hound him till he prays for death."

"Just be sure, Captain," Whit said, "that when you catch him, he doesn't chew you up. He's a fighter, this Black Hand, and he isn't afraid of dying. He'll give you a contest to remember. Depend on that."

"For a Reb, you speak mighty highly of this Indian," Captain Cloud rasped. "Your own tactics didn't do anything for you in the late war. At Five Forks my men had a hard time handling the droves of Rebs trying to surrender."

"I never fought there," Whit said sourly. "We fought you fair enough at Shiloh and at Vicksburg. Even near the end when I was up in Tennessee riding a nag that could barely trot, my company held its own. I fought the second day at Shiloh with two rounds for my musket and only a pinch of biscuit to eat. Wasn't superior tactics won the war for you, Captain. It was newer, better equipment, more manpower."

"And that's what will win here, too," Captain Cloud declared.

"You forget, though," Whit said, taking a sip of his rum. "We fought by the old rulebook, even when we knew we'd go down. Black Hand doesn't care an ounce for your rules. He makes his own. He's not afraid of what you'll do when it's over, because he plans to die fighting. It's hard dealing with a man who's not afraid, isn't it? What do you have to use against him? Nothing."

"Everybody's afraid of something," Captain Cloud objected. "We just have to find what it is."

"Good luck," Whit said, smiling.

Captain Cloud went on explaining his views on the campaign for the other officers, but Whit, having spoken his piece, slipped outside and walked under the stars. It was a bright, wonderfully crisp night, too pleasant to spend arguing with iron-headed Yanks.

"How's the cattle business?" Colonel Burnett asked from the porch.

"A little slow just now," Whit replied. "Once the ground dries out some, I think I'll round up some of the beeves, maybe trail a herd north to Abilene. They say a man can make a fortune with a successful drive."

"That's the word I get," the colonel agreed. "My brother-in-law brought two thousand head up from San Antonio last year. Did well on the sale, even though he lost two or three hundred on the way."

"Know what he got per head?" Whit asked.

"Said the buyers start at twenty-five. Good deal more if they're early."

"Range cow sells for maybe five dollars." Whit figured the profit in his head. "Twenty dollars profit for two thousand head . . ."

"Can make a man rich," the colonel said, lighting a cigar.

"I'd guess we could pull in five hundred easy," Whit said. "There'd be branding and gelding to get done, but we'd make a fine outfit, just the six of us that went after Black Hand's horses. Pick up a couple of others maybe. We'd make, what, ten thousand dollars? I've never even heard of a man having that much money, Colonel."

"You will," Colonel Burnett said confidently. "Once this Comanche problem is settled, this range is going to explode with big cattle operations. Those that get in early will have funds to buy more land. The day of the open range is coming to a close. Pretty soon you'll need titles to walk across the street."

"When is this Comanche problem going to be settled?" Whit asked. "You know they ride not two miles from here."

"Once we have enough men, we'll halt that."

"You've got enough men now," Whit grumbled. "It's not the number. It's how they're used. Big columns won't work. Black Hand reads your dust and goes elsewhere. Look at these hills. A man atop that ridge can watch you eat breakfast, Colonel. They know what you're doing before you do."

"How would you go about dealing with Black Hand?" Colonel Burnett asked.

"I'm not a soldier." Whit shook his head.

"If you were, how would you deal with him?"

"Like last time," Whit ventured. "I'd take his horses. Then I'd split into small forces and tie down the water holes. Sooner or later he'd come to me."

"That sounds logical. Tell you what. If you'll promise to keep me informed on what you know of Black Hand, I'll return the favor."

"I don't know that I can help you much."

"You already have. You're on my side, whether you know it or even want it, Macomb. You can't prosper and your family can't be safe so long as Black Hand is at large. He's got to go. We both know it."

"And?"

"Abilene's a long, hazardous journey, especially for a man unfamiliar with the hazards. My brother-in-law, Carter Greenhaw, is headed north already. I wrote him. He'd be willing to take five hundred steers on consignment. You'd get five dollars a head on pickup, and he'll split the profit at the railhead for any cattle that survive the trip."

"You mean we wouldn't trail the herd ourselves?" Whit asked.

"No, you'd only deliver them to Fort Griffin. I've arranged a contract for fifty steers to be delivered to the fort for their needs. You'd receive fifteen dollars a head for those."

"I don't understand," Whit said, scratching his chin. "Why are you being so good to me?"

"First, you saved me from some embarrassment concerning my horses last fall. Second, if you stay here, I've got an ally against the Comanches."

"I can't see how to refuse," Whit said, gazing down the creek where a few longhorns grazed. "When would I leave for Fort Griffin?"

"Three weeks' time. I'll arrange a cavalry escort. A full company if possible. I'm not planning to feed Black Hand."

"And my family?"

"I'll see a patrol watches your property."

"Then I'd say we've got a bargain," Whit said, shaking the colonel's hand. "This would be cash money, wouldn't it? Not just more land?"

"Cash money," the colonel said. "Paid on delivery at Fort Griffin."

Whit could hardly control his excitement. It wasn't until after the soldiers had left that he told Lucy all the details, but she sensed right away something extraordinary was going on.

"But won't that mean you'll be gone an awfully long time?" Lucy asked. "Fort Griffin is so far."

"A lot shorter than Abilene. I think we can manage it in four, five days."

"Each way," Tom said, joining the discussion. "Who's going to watch the farm while we're gone?"

"The colonel said he'll patrol the property. If you'd feel safer, Lucy, you could stay in town."

"If no one's here, they're sure to burn us out," she said, frowning. "Still, I'd feel better if someone were to stay."

"How would it be if I asked Ruben to ride out?" Whit suggested. "He'd enjoy some time with the boys, and he knows more about Indians than anyone I can think of."

"I'd like that," Lucy agreed. "And who's going to guard you on the road west?"

"Cavalry. Colonel Burnett promised a company."

"So there's really nothing to discuss, is there?" she concluded. "It sounds too good to be true."

"I know," Whit told her. "That bothers me some, too, but this promises to bring in seven hundred fifty dollars at Fort Griffin from the army, another twenty-five hundred for delivery of the five hundred steers. And if all reach Abilene, it'd be at least another five thousand."

With such figures to spout off, Whit had no trouble at all in interesting the Quinby brothers in a roundup. Tom gathered little Coley Adams and Chris McDermott to help. Several others drifted by to volunteer for the drive, but Whit chose only two, a one-armed ex-Confederate named Brad Sharp and Chris McDermott's sixteen-year-old cousin Steve, whose mother had arrived to help her sister Hannah at the Stratton House.

"I'll work for nothing, Mr. Macomb," young Steve had pleaded, "so long as you get me away from those dishes."

Most of the dozen men whom Whit rejected went off grumbling. Most had wanted their money in advance. Few appeared to be of the hardworking breed a cattle drive required. "Three of those men work dice tables down on Lost Creek," Charlie Quinby told Whit later. "We're well rid of them."

"I hope so," Whit agreed, "but we'll keep a

weather eye out for them just the same on the way home."

Once the crew was ready, Whit dispatched them in groups onto the range. Chasing down close to six hundred longhorns was hard work, especially since most were used to going their own way. They paid little attention to horses or men, and it was amusing to watch Coley Adams rope one of the longhorns, then try to pull the thousand-pound cow away from where it wanted to go. When Coley did get the longhorn's attention, often as not the beast would head for the youngster full speed, and Coley'd gallop away, his usually pinkish face white with panic. A stream of cussing would follow as the boy caught his breath.

Brad Sharp proved the master of rounding up longhorns. He'd still his horse by pressing inward with his knees, then crack a bullwhip with his good right arm. Cows discovered early it was best to avoid the sharp sting of that whip.

Collecting the cattle between Jones and Crooked creeks was a nightmare, but the really hard work followed. With cattle roaming freely across the range, the only way to prove ownership was to brand. Ruben had constructed six irons, each bearing a WM brand. The only novel feature was that it looked the same upside down.

Each day Whit sent his crews out early. A fire would be built, and each animal, from the meanest bull to the smallest calf, would be wrestled to the ground and branded. It sometimes took five of them to take the legs from under the more lively bulls, but an unbranded animal was free game for thieves.

Along with the branding came another unpleasant chore. Colonel Burnett had asked for steers, and nature didn't provide any such beast. As the cows were branded, they were herded back across the creeks. The largest and strongest of the bulls would be left for breeding. They would be chased off with the cows. Those unfortunates that remained were destined for the trail drive and the supper tables at Fort Griffin or further north. As they were branded, they were gelded as well.

"There are more pleasant things to spend a day doing," Ed remarked one afternoon. "Thank the Lord from now on we can do this to the calves."

Whit never recalled a harder three weeks, not even those final days at Vicksburg or the month he'd been holed up on the Powder River by Red Cloud's Sioux. He returned nightly bent in fifteen places, his entire body a single throbbing ache. He was sure no one had ever been as weary, and he wasn't nearly as sure what a fine price he was getting tor his labors.

The day they finished the branding, Whit made a rough count of the steers. They'd managed to collect almost six hundred, but it was decided to take them all in case there might be a few lost along the way.

"You know those cavalry boys," Charlie laughed. "They're apt to break one of those steers' legs just so they can have themselves a steak."

"If Black Hand shows up, you'll likely offer them their choice of beeves," Ed said, slapping his brother on the back. "A hundred Yank rifles will feel mighty good about the time those Comanches come charging down some ridge."

"Shoot, I'll even do their cooking," Coley said, wiping his forehead.

As the day of departure neared, Whit set to work making final preparations. He loaded a wagon with provisions and assigned Steve McDermott as driver. Coley proved a capable enough cook, and Whit abandoned thoughts of hiring an additional man. Finally, the steers were prodded across Jones Creek, through the Trinity at Comanche Crossing, then southwesterly until they joined the cavalry escort on the old Fort Belknap road. At the head of the column was the person Whit least wished to see there.

"Well, Mr. Macomb, it appears I'm to protect you from the Comanches," Captain Cloud said, saluting with spotless white gloves.

"We'll see who needs protecting," Ed grumbled.

"That's enough," Whit said as the captain glared angrily. "We've got our own jobs to do. Let's attend them."

As the captain split his company into van and rear guards, plus an escort for each flank, Whit whispered his own agreement.

"But he's all we've got, Ed," Whit added. "And I don't want him getting himself lost along the road. We've put too much time and effort in to wind up empty-handed."

Ed reluctantly agreed, and Whit rode to where Lucy and the boys waited in her buggy to bid farewell.

"You boys take care of your mama," Whit told Billy and Ben, touching their shoulders fondly, then shaking their hands.

"And me?" Lucy said

"I promise to come home," Whit said, kissing her lightly on the cheek. "It won't take eight years this time."

"It better not," she warned.

Chapter Twelve

The old Belknap military road sounded far grander than the thin line of sandy ruts that cut its way through the buffalo grass of the range westward out of Jacksboro. Except for stagecoaches or army supply wagons, only rare horsemen traveled its dusty length. Those familiar with the area preferred to journey along the creeks and rivers that cut across west-central Texas.

To call it a road at all required a powerful imagination. Ruben once described it as seventy-five miles of arroyo and prickly pear carved along the fringe of the great southern buffalo range.

There were some advantages of the Belknap road, though. It provided a wide route, perfect for shepherding six hundred steers. It generally kept to the high ground, offering a view of the surrounding countryside. Most important, it wound its way through most of the settlements that lay between Jacksboro and Fort Griffin, meaning the buffalo and its pursuing Comanches stayed clear. Usually.

But the long cloud of dust raised by the cattle and the horsemen could be seen for miles. It wasn't long before a line of bare-chested riders appeared on a nearby ridge.

"There!" Tom shouted, pointing to the Indians.

Captain Cloud waved the northern flank riders toward the Comanches. Whit hurried to halt the deployment, but the young lieutenant heading the column was already directing a charge.

"Captain!" Whit yelled as he rode furiously toward the cavalryman. "Captain Cloud!"

But when Whit pulled his chestnut stallion to a stop beside the captain, he found the vanguard preparing to join the pursuit.

"Captain, please," Whit gasped, fighting to catch his breath.

"This is none of your business, Macomb," Cloud said, turning his attention back to the three or four Comanches on the distant ridge. "I won't let this opportunity slip away."

"What opportunity?" Whit asked. "Can't you see there's just a handful of them over there? If you're going to charge after each one that pops up, all you'll do is exhaust your men and horses and you won't catch any Comanches."

"I tell you what, Macomb," the captain said, waving the vanguard toward the distant ridge. "You watch your cattle, and I'll tend to the Indians."

The captain then spurred his horse, galloping off to catch the column.

"Fool ironhead!" Whit said, shaking his head. "Leaves us with half an escort while he's off chasing a handful of decoys!"

Whit returned to his companions still grumbling.

"Wish we'd run across a few more of those type Yanks in the war," Ed said, spitting. "Those kind get their whole command shot to pieces, then pick up a promotion and a sob story in the newspapers."

"He won't find anything up there," Whit said, slapping his knee. "But I don't suppose Black Hand's got enough interest in us to face the fifty or so bluecoats still here."

"Wait till the other fifty go romping off the other way," Ed said, pointing toward another pair of Indian scouts atop a hill to the south.

Whit dashed immediately for the southern outriders, twenty men who rode behind a grizzled old sergeant.

"Sergeant?" Whit asked, gazing at the pair of youthful Comanches a quarter mile away.

"I see 'em," the sergeant said, biting on a square of tobacco. "You want I should do something about 'em?"

"No," Whit sighed with relief. "I wanted to warn you against chasing shadows."

"See these stripes?" The sergeant pointed to the three chevrons on his sleeve. "I didn't get 'em goin' to school. I earned 'em chasin' you Rebs across half the South. I've tangled with a few Indians in my time, too. That right, boys?"

The soldiers raised a quick cheer, and Whit smiled.

"I was a sergeant once myself," Whit said, wiping the sweat from his forehead. "I made a few mistakes, though, and they promoted me to captain."

It was the sergeant's turn to laugh now, and half the column joined in.

"Where'd you serve, Reb?"

"In the west, at Shiloh, Corinth, then Vicksburg. Later on I rode with the cavalry in Tennessee and Kentucky."

"We'll have to have ourselves a talk," the sergeant said. "I was at Shiloh myself."

"I'm Whit Macomb," Whit said, extending his hand.

"Al Douglas," the sergeant responded.

"I'll leave you to your duties, Sergeant," Whit said, turning back toward his crew.

Captain Cloud sent detachments out five times that day, but not a single Indian was brought back. When Whit motioned his crew to bed down the animals along the banks of a shallow creek, the captain began deploying his soldiers in a giant circle around the herd.

"That'll make night guard a little easier," Chris pointed out as the dusty riders gathered near the supply wagon.

"Don't you believe it," Whit said. "We'll keep

our eyes open. I'm a long way from trusting this ironhead to protect us from anything.''

Sure enough, in spite of Captain Cloud's pickets, Comanches stole three army horses. The cavalrymen ended up borrowing from the ponies Whit had brought along as relief.

That second day on the trail seemed to last an eternity. It was hot and dry and dusty. Whit would have given half his arm for a dip in the crisp, cool water of the Trinity.

Evening was even worse. Three times Cloud's pickets fired off shots, and the longhorns nearly bolted.

''Your men keep firing, you'll have a hundred thousand pounds of hoof and horn rolling over your camp,'' Whit finally warned the captain. ''Keep your wits. Nobody's going to bother you here. Watch the stock. These ones you're running across now are only boys out to prove they've got the gumption to be men.''

''And just where did you learn to be a military genius?'' Captain Cloud snapped.

''I never claimed I was anything but a Texas farmboy,'' Whit answered, growing slightly crimson. ''But I've fought Comanches since I was five years old. I served in the army, mine and yours.''

''Where?''

''Shiloh the first time. Fort Reno on the Powder River last time.''

''I remember Shiloh,'' the captain said, laughing. ''We whipped you Rebs that day!''

''You weren't there,'' Whit said, spitting the bad taste from his mouth. ''You don't know.''

As Whit paced angrily beside his blankets that

night, Sergeant Douglas appeared with a youthful corporal.

"I heard the captain," Sergeant Douglas said. "I remember how it was. You Rebs with your screamin' ran us out of our camps. I lost a pair of good leather boots that first mornin'. My brother Dan fell in the Hornet's Nest. Me, I half hoped you boys'd reach the landin' so we could call an end to the whole fuss. Some good boys died that day."

"On both sides," Whit agreed, sitting beside the embers of the campfire.

"I was a drummer," the corporal said. "Only twelve. They shot my drum. You Rebs, I mean. Was a good drum, made up in New York. We patched it, but it was never any good after that."

"Young Chris McDermott lost his brother in the fighting," Whit said, motioning to the mop of blond hair lying five feet away. "Those were hard days. We made a charge at Corinth . . . was pure stupid. Got the regiment shot to pieces, and it was for nothing. I guess most of the officers died that day. That's when they made me a captain. Ran out of fools who'd take the reins, so to speak."

"Know what I remember best?" the young corporal asked.

"No, what?" Whit asked.

"The nights at Vicksburg. We'd start singing, and then you Rebs would answer. Pretty soon the war would be a thousand miles away."

The corporal swung a guitar out and began playing softly. Tom Morgan rose from his blankets and hummed along.

"You play, boy?" the corporal asked.

"Used to," Tom answered, crawling over to the fire.

"Well, go ahead and take a turn. I'm Pat Hodges," the corporal said, smiling.

"Tom Morgan," Tom said, taking the guitar. "Could be I'm a little rusty."

But in truth Tom played quite well. He started out with a quiet lullaby, then followed with an old Welsh ballad.

"Shame we can't sit down with those Comanches like this," Corporal Hodges said. "I'll bet we could settle things."

"Maybe," Whit said. "There's not much to settle really, except who's got a right to this land. We both can't have it. As long as we try to occupy it, the Comanches'll fight. If we leave, they'll settle down for a time."

"They can have the whole of Texas as far as I'm concerned," the corporal said. "It's too hot and dry and dusty. There aren't enough shade trees, and the bugs eat a man right out of his skin."

"But when you sit out here on a night like this, you feel like God's watchin'," Sergeant Douglas sighed. "When my hitch is up, I think I'd like to take a try at runnin' some cattle, build me a little ranch, find a sassy little wife, and raise some kids."

"A fair ambition," Whit agreed.

The third day seemed different from the start. The sun cast an eerie glow at dawn, a haunting shade of scarlet that alarmed the soldiers.

"Blood red," Ed commented. "Time for battle."

It certainly seemed so. Early on, two long columns of Comanches appeared on each side of the herd, stepping slowly, patiently so as to keep pace. Leading the right-hand column was a warrior on a brown speckled pony. His shield bore a distinctive black hand.

"They're on the ridge, too," Tom pointed out.

"Must be the whole bunch," Whit said, sighing. "I count maybe sixty."

"They going to attack?" Coley asked, riding beside Whit and staring nervously at the Indians.

"That'd be a fool's move," Whit said. "What's to be gained? The soldiers would kill a couple of dozen at least. No, it's just Black Hand's way of letting us know he's around."

Captain Cloud didn't view it that way, though. He took command of the right and sent a lieutenant to lead the left. Amid a bugle fanfare, the cavalry charged.

"You boys watch yourselves," Whit said, doing his best to organize his men for defense. He sent Ed and Charlie to guard the rear with young Steve McDermott. The exposed right was held by Brad Sharp, Chris, and Tom. Whit watched the left with Coley Adams.

"Just relax, son," Whit said, pulling his Winchester from its saddle scabbard. "Just hold yourself ready. If riders head our way, you let me take the first. Aim for the second. Understand?"

Coley nodded nervously and pulled the long rifle out.

Captain Cloud, meanwhile, managed to engage himself in a game of blind man's bluff. The swirling dust hid everything, and, if not for the sounds of a hundred rifles and carbines discharging, Whit never would have known a battle was taking place.

The only real threat to the herd came from four warriors on the left. They screamed to high heaven, then raced their ponies toward the longhorns.

"Take the second," Whit reminded Coley before shooting the lead rider from the saddle. Coley fired three times rapidly, hitting the second Comanche in the arm. Whit then knocked the third from his pony. The fourth turned back.

"Fair shooting, Coley," Whit said as two of the Indians staggered to their feet and limped away. The first remained frozen as he'd fallen.

The cavalry accomplished little besides wasting half its ammunition. A single Comanche corpse was found on the far hillside, and three bluecoats were hit, two seriously enough that they were put in the supply wagon. The third seemed fine at first, then fell stone-cold dead an hour later.

"Gather up, men, and we'll go after them," Captain Cloud ordered as squad after squad of horsemen returned.

"They've got nothing left," Sergeant Douglas explained. "You chase that devil with the black hand on his shield over that next hill, you'll find him. Yes, sir, you'll find him staring you right in the facc, singing your death with his rifle."

"Sergeant!" the captain barked.

"Somebody's got to say it," said the sergeant. "This is a game with 'em, Captain. Let's get these cows to the fort. We can go after 'em all we want on the way back."

That would have been Whit's suggestion, too, but the captain would have none of it. The weary troopers mounted up and chased Black Hand's shadow another ten miles.

Whit made camp past the old Belknap Indian agency on the Clear Fork of the Brazos. The cattle drank greedily, and Whit dove into the water with his crew. Later that evening the returning soldiers took advantage of the cool water to bathe away their troubles.

"Lost two more men up there," Sergeant Douglas grumbled as he sat beside Whit's fire. "Whoever signed that man's commission ought to dig the graves."

"Your men look in bad shape," commented Whit.

"Men and horses both," the sergeant agreed. "But we'll be at the fort tomorrow, I expect."

"Could be," Whit said as Corporal Hodges arrived. The corporal and Tom took turns playing old camp songs, and the night filled with the tired voices of troopers and drovers.

"Tomorrow that Comanche demon can have us if he wants," Sergeant Douglas said, kicking a rock across the flat land.

"No, he'll be headed back to the buffalo valleys," Whit said. "Too close to the fort for him now. Too far from home."

Morning found it as Whit predicted. Though the cavalry escort trudged along slowly to the rear, Whit urged the stock onward until they were safely approaching the hillside dominated by the stone buildings of Fort Griffin.

Chapter Thirteen

The cavalry post at Fort Griffin seemed bleak and austere compared to the green parade ground and neat rows of picket barracks at Fort Richardson. The stone buildings towered above the surrounding landscape. A scarcity of shade left the post baking in the bright sunlight. Even in spring the quarters were warm and uncomfortable. Whit hated to imagine the inferno that summer would bring.

Below the fort sprawled a thriving little town, feeding itself on the whims of soldiers and buffalo hunters. Piano music drifted across the plain, mixing with boisterous talk to give the place an aura of unrespectability.

"I see you spotted The Flat," Sergeant Douglas said, pointing toward the town. "The first ones to set up their whiskey inns and dance halls named it Fort Griffin Town, but nobody calls it that now. Isn't up to town rank, if you ask me. But if you're lookin' for a bit of a good time, The Flat's the place to go."

Whit had little desire to go anywhere but home. After delivering the promised fifty head to the Fort Griffin quartermaster, Whit ordered the remaining five hundred to be taken to where Carter Greenhaw's herd grazed on the prairie nearby. Greenhaw's count found an overage of twelve steers.

"Be glad to take them along, too," the cattleman said. "Truth is, I wish I had another five hundred. Don't suppose any of your crew'd care to come along? I'd pay them for their efforts."

"I need most of them to work my place," Whit explained, "but if you've got no feeling against a one-handed ex-Confederate, I'll send you one good one."

Except for suggesting to Brad Sharp that there might be a spot on the trail crew, Whit kept silent when handing out the promised wages, a pair of twenty-dollar gold pieces plus a share of the profits for Ed and Charlie. In addition, Whit entrusted Al Douglas with funds for each of the soldiers to enjoy a free drink at one of The Flat's saloons.

"When do you plan to ride back?" Charlie asked as Whit led the way toward the booming music of The Flat.

"Right now," Whit told them. "I won't rest easy till I see Lucy and the boys again."

"Thought you said the colonel was sending patrols to watch the place," Tom said.

"So he told me," Whit explained, "but I kind of lost my faith in the cavalry here lately."

"Well, can't see as I blame you," Charlie said, "but I hope you won't hold it against Ed and me if we celebrate a little. We haven't had this much hard money in ten years."

"Save a little of it for later," Whit said as the Quinbys turned away.

"You wouldn't mind too much if Steve and I had a look around over there, either, would you?" Chris asked, eyeing the shantytown eagerly. "Those soldiers told some mighty wild tales about the goings-on there."

"I need Steve to drive the supply wagon," Whit pointed out.

"If it's fair to you, Mr. Macomb, I'll drive it on back tomorrow," Steve said. "I'll come now if you want, though. You've been more than square with me, and I'll abide by your terms."

"See you stay close to Ed and Charlie," Whit warned. "Town like that attracts its share of bad ones."

"Yes, sir," Chris said as he led his cousin toward the closest of the saloons.

"Well?" Whit gazed at Coley and Tom. "Don't you want to go, too?"

"Well, I was thinking on it," Coley said, scratching his ear. "You won't tell my mama, will you?"

"Go on," Whit laughed. "You, too, Tom."

"Somebody ought to look after Coley, him being small like he is."

"I'll see you back home," Whit said as he waved them off.

Afterward, as he rode eastward all alone, he regretted not being free to hit the saloons with his companions, sing a few songs, or dance with the redheads. But that was something he'd swapped for the uneasy feeling in his stomach, for the fear that something might happen to Lucy or one of the boys. Once Whit had gotten around to it, he'd sunk his roots deep.

Whit rode alone for little more than three miles. Someone hailed him from behind, and he turned in time to discover Tom and Coley Adams charging after him.

"Couldn't spend forty dollars that quick," Whit said as the boys joined him.

"Ah, they said Coley was too young," Tom said, grinning. "Me, I couldn't very well let him hang around outside."

"They said *he* was too young," Coley said, pointing at Tom. "They called *me* too little."

"Guess they don't know much about judging men, huh?" Whit chuckled.

"Couldn't," Coley said, taking off his hat and smoothing his long blond hair. "Those folks wouldn't know a longhorn from a buffalo chip."

"Besides," Tom said, nudging his horse into motion, "we couldn't very well let you go riding home all by yourself, not with all that money."

"Sorry to disappoint you boys, but the better part of that money's in the form of a bank draft,"

Whit explained. "Safer to carry and a whole lot easier on my poor old horse."

"Sure does take the adventure out of it," Tom complained. "But it might keep us clear of road agents, I guess."

Whit agreed, though Coley told them a dozen times how he'd handle any outlaws who happened along.

In the next three days, they saw almost nothing on the Belknap road. A team of wagons hauling supplies to The Flat passed them the second day, and a few solitary longhorns appeared once or twice. There were no signs of Comanches.

"Glad there aren't," Tom said as he slipped between his blankets the second night.

Whit wasn't so sure. It had been reassuring to know Black Hand was nearby. That way the Indian couldn't be back raiding the farm or tormenting Lucy.

Once Whit began to detect familiar ridges and streams, he left the road and headed cross-country. The western half of the county was crawling with maverick cattle, and a herd of mustangs rode past them south of where Plum Creek emptied into the Trinity. As they passed the ruins of the old Carson place, Whit paused.

"That cabin's been that way all my life," Coley said. "Chris and I were out here once last summer."

"The Carson farm," Whit mumbled. "I used to come here with my sister Katie. There'd be singing and dancing . . . more noise than you could imagine. Girls dressed in fine things, with ribbons in their hair; boys scrubbed and their hair cut. We had some high times."

"I remember your sister," Tom said, his face growing pale. "Ruben had her make me a pair of pants just after Mama and Papa got . . . just after they died. She was real pretty."

"Yes," Whit sighed. But there was no point to remembering. They'd be home soon, and Lucy's smile would chase away the sadness.

Crossing Cameron Creek onto the Macomb farm, Whit sent Tom to ride with Coley to the Adams place.

"I haven't seen any sign of trouble, but it's better not to be riding this country alone," Whit told them.

"What about you?" Tom asked.

"Oh, I'm never alone once I'm home," Whit explained. "Besides, I've got a couple of stops to make."

"I understand," Tom said, nodding.

It was late afternoon by the time Whit had ridden past Hadley's Spring, visited the old house, and forded the Trinity at Comanche Crossing. Relieved to see no fresh tracks in the sand, he splashed his way across Jones Creek and called to Lucy. He was met by the coldest silence he had ever known.

"Lucy? Billy? Ben?" Whit called again. "Ruben?"

Except for an old crow fluttering around in the upper branches of a willow, there was no sound.

Maybe they've gone to town, Whit told himself. But as he climbed the hill and gazed on the charred fragments that had been the house and barn, he knew that wasn't so.

"Lucy!" Whit screamed, sliding off his horse and racing around the farmhouse. A Comanche lance stood in front of where the door had been, and Whit kicked it angrily away.

"Lucy? Billy? Ben?"

There was nothing save the twin chimneys of the house, the burned timbers of the barn. Whit bent over and picked up a toy wagon of Billy's. Except for blackened edges, the toy seemed little changed. Whit spun the wheels and called out again.

Hogs rooted in the ashes of the barn. Chickens fluttered around the shambles of the coop. Clothing was scattered. It was like the other times. Whit felt his insides grow stiff and cold. The fingers of his left hand ached.

"No!" he screamed, shaking furiously. "Not again!"

The animals fled from the barn, and even the old crow grew quiet. Across Jones Creek atop a low hill appeared a single bare-chested rider. He held no shield, and his horse was hidden by brush, but Whit knew who it was.

"Black Hand!" Whit shouted so that the words echoed through the valley. The Indian raised a hand, then vanished into the scarlet evening.

You've had your vengeance, Whit thought, staring at the shambles of his home. But I'm still here! And I'll stay, too!

Whit heard footsteps nearby and turned quickly. Before him walked the shadow of a lone figure, a slightly built youth with sweaty blond hair falling across his forehead. Whit trembled. Was it an apparition? Was he gazing at the ghost of another Whit Macomb, a boy who'd returned one day to discover his father dead, his home destroyed?

"I came when I heard." The shadow spoke with a familiar voice. "I saw Ruben."

The words were Whit's own, but the voice was different. Whit blinked his eyes and found himself looking at young Tom Morgan.

"They're all right, Whit," Tom said. "Ruben got them into town before the burning."

"Thank God," Whit said, stepping over and leaning against a nearby post oak. "I thought . . ."

"No, they're all fine," Tom said, helping Whit sit down. "The Comanches must have ridden straight here after they saw they couldn't get our cattle. Close to thirty. Ruben stood them off, but they were bound to come back the next day. He got Lucy and the kids out. The cavalry never did come."

"It's my fault," Whit rumbled. "I should've known."

"You did what you had to," Tom said. "You always do. Ruben told me that. Why don't you come back to town with me, see Mrs. Macomb and the boys? Then tomorrow we can start rebuilding."

"Sure," Whit said, sighing.

Together they mounted their horses and headed south down the Buffalo Springs road.

Chapter Fourteen

Whit greeted Lucy in the parlor of the Stratton House. For a minute they simply stared into each other's sad eyes. Then they embraced, held each other until they were seemingly one being.

"So, what do we do now?" Lucy finally asked.

"Rebuild," he told her. "We can afford to, at least. I've never heard of a man who had more than a thousand dollars to his name without a roof over his head."

"We saved what we could, Whit."

"You saved what was important," he said, spying the boys in the doorway. "Don't you suppose a fine pair of young men like these ought to at least say welcome home to their papa?"

Billy trotted over and reached his arms around Whit's waist. Little Ben hugged one leg. Whit drew them both close.

"Well! You boys finally got to see some Indians. Care to see more of them?" Whit asked.

The boys shook their heads, and Whit laughed.

"You're serious about rebuilding the house?" Lucy asked.

"Yes, but this time we'll do it differently," Whit told her. "We'll put in a basement, and the walls will be of stone. Black Hand's burned his last Macomb house."

"Stone?"

"It's little different from what they've done at the fort. It's going to be hard work, but we can get it done. With the cattle on their way to market, we've got little else to occupy our time."

"You'll put in a wooden floor this time, I hope."

"Even for the basement?" Whit asked.

Lucy nodded, then began making a list of other changes.

"And finally," she said, "I think Tom ought to have his own room. He's entitled to a few days free of pranks."

"I don't mind," Tom objected.

"Nonsense," Lucy said. "We might as well balance the place. Two other bedrooms opposite the sitting room."

"Two?" Whit asked.

"Well, I certainly don't plan on sharing our room. And come late summer, we'll be needing a place for our daughter."

"Daughter?"

"Well, I'm due to have a girl, don't you think? Two boys seem more than enough."

"You're expecting?" Whit asked.

"August or September," Lucy told him.

"Well, that's fine," he said, smiling brightly. "Oh, Lucy, that's just fine."

"Of course, it's a little early to be thinking of names or knitting clothes, but I think you ought to add the room to the house."

He kissed her, then threw his hat in the air.

"Well," he said, "that settles one thing. You and the boys will stay in town till I get the house finished. It's clearly no time for you to be running around dodging Comanche arrows. You haven't got this whole place rented, have you?"

"No fear of that," Lucy remarked. "Too much competition down the creek."

"Once Ed and Charlie get back, we'll start building. I'll have them stay out there at night. I'll ride in to be with you and the boys."

"That would be nice," she said, "But if you feel the need to stay on the ranch, we'll understand. It's too far to ride twice every day."

"Somebody does it with the eggs anyway," Whit pointed out. "I wouldn't want you running off with old Atwood from the mercantile now, would I?"

"I'd worry about Judge Baker, if it was me," Lucy said, laughing.

It was half a week before the Quinby brothers

escorted the supply wagon back into Jacksboro. Chris and Steve McDermott jumped down and began telling Tom a hundred tales at once, but the presence of their mothers quickly put a stop to that. Meanwhile, Whit filled in Ed and Charlie on the burning of the ranch.

"I worried about that," Ed said, slapping his hat against the wagon. "Just like our place."

"We had to make the cattle sale," Whit said. "I hate to lose that barn, but it happens. The stock can be rounded up later. Right now I want to start on the house."

"We can get a load of lumber from the sawmill," Charlie offered.

"First we need to get some powder," Whit told them.

"Powder?" Ed asked.

"This time I'm building out of stone. We'll blast out a basement. Then we can build walls two stories high."

"Kind of like one of those storybook castles, huh?" Charlie joshed.

"Sure," Whit said. "Perfect for holding off cavalry, especially the kind that waves lances and carries torches."

Whit talked Ruben into supervising the blasting. Two stonemasons who'd worked on the post hospital at Fort Richardson were hired to work on the house. Whit devoted his efforts to digging out the balance of the basement after Ruben blew a forty-foot hole in the rocky hillside.

Once the house was laid out, the masons mixed a pasty mortar and began laying the foundation beams. Whit and the Quinbys laid the basement floor and raised the support columns for the walls and upper floors. Room was left for a stairway, and two matching chimneys rose skyward from the basement.

"You're going to have yourself a fine place here, Mr. Macomb," George Winters, one of the masons, observed. "I built myself a house like this down south."

"Have a lot of Comanches there, too?" Tom asked.

"No, son, just a wife who wants a big house," Winters hooted.

As the walls began taking shape, Whit spotted the first Comanche scouts, two boys no older than Tom. Whit walked their way with a notion to catch them, but the Indians vanished in the wink of an eye.

"They learn early, those Comanches," Ed said, shaking his head.

Since returning from Fort Griffin, Captain Cloud had kept mounted patrols scouring the countryside for some sign of Black Hand, but the wily Comanche was always elsewhere.

"A man can't be that lucky," Sergeant Douglas complained while visiting the ranch on one such patrol. "He's got a trick, no doubt about it."

"Could be," Whit said, sharing a glance with Ed Quinby. "Maybe Ed and I ought to have a look around. When do you usually head out?"

"Eight sharp every morning," the sergeant growled. "That's part of the problem right there. I told the captain he ought to be more unpredictable, but you know these West Point types. They have to stick to their procedures. If old Grant had stuck to rules, Robert E. Lee'd be president now."

Whit laughed at the remark. But he took Douglas's words seriously. An hour before dawn the following morning Whit and Ed crept along the Trinity, keeping an eye out for signs of Comanches. Even before the sun was above the horizon, a pair of Indians rode past, heading for the high slope of Squaw Mountain.

"Old Black Hand's no fool," Ed said. "He's got himself a lookout up there. You can watch every inch of that fort from Squaw Mountain. Gives him fair warning of the cavalry's approach."

"Could be we can do something to change that," Whit replied.

When Captain Cloud rode northward that morning, Whit and Ed met him with news of the Squaw Mountain lookout.

"You admire this Black Hand greatly, don't you?" the captain sneered. "The way you talk, you'd think he was Napoleon and Winfield Scott reborn. Lookouts! Decoys! You're only fooling yourselves. He's only been lucky so far. We'll deal with him soon."

"You keep at it the way you have been, he'll be lucky for a long time yet," Ed said bitterly. "We know how they fight, Yank! We've been killing each other for a lifetime."

"You give these Comanches entirely too much credit," Captain Cloud declared. "It's like the people in Washington treated Stonewall Jackson and Bedford Forrest. The mere mention of those names had everyone terrified. Well, they met their end, and so will this Black Hand."

"Bedford Forrest fought till the end," Whit reminded the captain. "No one forced him to sign the terms, either. And Stonewall Jackson fell to his own men."

It was the last remark Whit would make on the subject. Disappointed, he led Ed back to the house and resumed work. Later that week Whit passed on his information to Colonel Burnett at the Stratton House.

"We'll post guards on that hill," the colonel said, smiling. "By thunder, that Cloud's a fool. I'll vary the departures."

"You know you won't catch Black Hand till you decide to lay an ambush," Whit sighed as he gazed sleepily out the front window. "He's too slippery to run down. He's got to be trapped like the fox he is. Lured by tempting bait, then swarmed upon."

"I'm afraid that's easier said than done," Colonel Burnett said.

"I fear you're right," Whit agreed.

Nevertheless the cavalry started maintaining night watches from Squaw Mountain. The patrols left at different times, and often changed direction once they set out. In a single week the Sixth Cavalry spotted more Comanches than in the previous six months. Four Indians were captured, and a fifth was shot dead.

Whit had little time to follow the cavalry's exploits. He had a house to build. Ruben discovered regular windows wouldn't work, so Whit designed a sort of double window, two sliding panels with glass panes that could be drawn back on their hinges. A thick sliding oak shutter could then be dropped into place to protect the occupants of the house. Each shutter had a narrow crosscut in it, allowing a rifle to be fired outside.

Once the first-floor windows were fitted, it was time to build the stairway and second floor. As nails were hammered into place and beams installed, the Comanche scouts across the creek would stare in disbelief. The stone walls already towered over the surrounding landscape. As the masons built the second story, Whit felt himself standing in an ancient Roman watchtower gazing down on the barbarian hordes of the north. A cannon might still shatter its walls, but nothing else could hope to threaten the place. Comanches carried no cannon.

Captain Cloud rode by to inspect the building one afternoon as Whit and Tom started the second-floor windows.

"Looks as if you're building your own fort here, Macomb," the captain jeered, gazing upward.

"I am," Whit snapped. "I mean to stay here."

The following night the Quinbys chased off a small party of raiders who tried to burn the floorboards. No damage was done except to one of the young Comanches, who lost a moccasin to Charlie Quinby.

It wasn't much longer before the masons finished the walls. They also built a three-foot stone wall surrounding the front of the house. Ruben constructed an iron gate in front with the familiar WM emblem overhead. Enclosed within the wall was the vital water well.

Whit used the ash shingles that had worked so

well before for a roof. It was the most vulnerable part of the structure, but by using green wood, the chance of a fire spreading rapidly was reduced. Being an additional twelve feet in height made the roof slightly harder to hit, too.

Aside from building hog pens and repairing the chicken coop, Whit had the old corrals replaced and strengthened. Instead of a barn, a sort of ramshackle stable was put together to shield the horses come winter. When all was finished, Whit rode alone along Jones Creek until he spotted Black Hand's scouts.

"Now, Black Hand!" Whit screamed. "Now come and chase me off my land! Your time's over, old friend. Finished. Hunt the buffalo while you can. Enjoy the summer sky. Soon it will all be over."

As Whit turned back toward the house, Tom Morgan joined him.

"You must really hate that Indian," Tom said, shaking his head. "I've never seen your eyes so full of fire."

"He burned my home, endangered my family," Whit growled.

"I hate all the Comanches. I don't know which one murdered my family, but I still wake up nights remembering how they used their knives on my brother Mike, how they killed Annie because she cried!"

"I'm bitter, too, Tom," Whit said, reaching over to touch the youngter's trembling arm. "But hate? No, I don't hate him. Truth is I understand him better than a prim and proper bluecoat like Captain Cloud. Sometimes I even admire Black

Hand. He's fighting the good fight, the battle against all the odds. It takes a special kind of man to stay with it when he knows he can't win."

"He can't?" Tom asked.

"No, and I'd guess he knows that. He could ride off and make a good life for himself, but he's Black Hand, a Comanche. To him that means he has to be true to his people, to his heritage. If he leaves Jack County, the Comanches will lose this land forever. Yes, we're alike, Black Hand and me. We both love this land, know it for what it is, a hard, unrelenting place that never really yields itself up to anyone. I suppose we're two of a kind. The trouble is that only one of us can win."

"Are you sure it'll be you?"

"I've got all the odds on my side," Whit said. "One of these days the cavalry's going to wake up and figure out how to fight the Comanches. I've got Winchester rifles that give me fifteen shots to his one. I can stay warm on the coldest December night, and I've got all the beef I can eat walking this range. Black Hand's people freeze all winter, and if they lose their foodstocks, they starve."

"When do you suppose it'll be over?" Tom asked.

"Maybe soon," Whit said, nudging his horse into a trot. "Maybe never. Who knows?"

Chapter Fifteen

Now that the house was rebuilt, Whit brought Lucy and the boys out for an inspection tour.

"This is a home?" Lucy asked as Billy chased Ben up the stairs. "Stone walls and wooden floors don't offer much comfort."

"It's safe, though," Whit said, pounding the solid stone walls.

"Of course. Who'd want to take it away from us?"

Immediately she set to work arranging imaginary furniture and making notations in a small book.

"I haven't had time to build much of anything," Whit explained. "I got the beds put in. Later I'll put together . . ."

"It's not for you to bother yourself with," Lucy told him. "What we need can be bought at the mercantile. We've got the money. You told me that yourself. I'll pick out a hutch, a table, and some chairs. We'll need some chests for the bedrooms. When you have time, fashion me some shelves. A pantry would be nice. And I'll measure the windows for curtains."

"I'd wait a moment or two on that," Whit told her. "The shutters will keep out the light, and they don't burn as nicely."

"Burn?" she questioned, resting her hands on her hips.

"The Comanches haven't gone away, Lucy. We've just made it tough for them to bother us."

"I suppose you're right," she frowned. "But in time I'll want to paper the walls with something cheerful."

"How about Confederate bonds?"

She shook her head and pretended anger, but Whit spied a smile. As Whit and the boys stuffed fresh straw in the mattresses that afternoon, he couldn't conceal how glad he was to have them there. At the same time a general uneasiness haunted the farm.

Furniture wasn't the only thing Whit hauled to the farm. He also brought a case of Winchesters. The rifles and boxes of shells were stored beside each window, ready at a moment's notice. Whit allowed no one to venture past Jones Creek without a rifle, and one of the Quinbys stood watch each night.

Most of the farm's regular income came from delivering beef, pork, eggs, milk, and butter to Jacksboro. Butter and eggs had become particularly dear, and they brought the price of a side of beef most days. Whit turned the chickens over to Billy and Ben. Tom Morgan milked the six cows Whit kept on hand, and Lucy churned the butter and kept it in the cool basement larder.

Whit and the Quinbys, occasionally joined by Tom Morgan, little Coley Adams, and the McDermott cousins, occupied themselves running down wild ponies on the far western range. Ruben always found a good market for Jack County ponies, and Whit felt best when he had twenty mounts around for the farm's need.

In late May Colonel Burnett contracted for another fifty head of cattle. The beeves were to be delivered to Fort Griffin as before, the sole difference being that the price had risen to twenty dollars a head.

"And an escort?" Whit asked.

"A squad should be sufficient," the colonel said. "Sergeant and ten men."

"Mind if I pick the sergeant?" Whit asked.

"Have someone in mind, do you?" Colonel Burnett asked.

"Sergeant Douglas impressed me last time out. Can you send him along?"

Colonel Burnett agreed, and Whit rounded up his crew. Fifty head posed nothing like the same problems the earlier herd had presented. Whit took

Tom and the boys along, but the Quinbys were left to look after the ranch. With Sergeant Douglas along, the journey went smoothly. The few Comanche scouts who appeared were ignored, and the one time Black Hand rushed the camp, Sergeant Douglas's steady soldiers sent the Indians reeling with a well-directed volley.

Whit returned a week later with crisp greenbacks in his pocket to find the farm unchanged. The next day, though, as he rode along the Trinity, he spotted the tracks of as many as fifty unshod ponies.

"Summer's raiding time," Ed Quinby said, staring hard at the far hillside. "Old Black Hand will have gathered his strength. We're apt to get his attention soon."

But though the warm weather brought an increase in Comanche activity throughout the county, Whit himself noticed fewer scouts spying from the far bank of Jones Creek. Charlie and Ed almost never had to deal with night visitors, and even while hunting mustangs, Whit wasn't bothered.

The crisp June sunlight helped to chase away some of Lucy's gloom. She appeared spry and cheerful in spite of carrying the child, and Whit entertained the boys with stories of the frontier and swimming races across the creek. Remembering a rope swing his brother had always treasured, Whit built a similar one under the branch of a giant white oak that leaned across the creek. Billy and Ben laughed with delight as they swung high in the air, then jumped into the cool waters of the creek below.

Tom often took the boys to the river on fishing excursions, and more than once a channel cat or a plump bass brought welcome relief from the steady diet of pork and beef.

Colonel Burnett worked his men hard that June, sending patrol after patrol across the rolling terrain in search of Black Hand's Comanches. As a result, Lucy and other ladies arranged entertainments on Friday and Saturday nights, some for the officers, some for the men. Often Colonel Burnett and the officers would gather in the parlor to smoke their cigars and exchange polite conversation. Corporal Hodges, joined by Tom Morgan, would play the guitar and sing sad melodies.

More often than not, Whit would gather Billy and Ben to escape the monotony of the parlor and walk down to the hog pens where Tom and the corporal played for the soldiers. The boys would hum along as best they could with the melancholy refrains of each song, and the soldiers would share news from home or memories. It was an eerily quiet, enchanted time.

"You figure we maybe made a mistake fighting those Yanks?" Billy asked one night as Whit tucked the boy in. "They seem nice enough."

"All people are pretty much alike when you take the time to know them," Whit said, moving over to Ben and tucking the smaller boy in as well.

"Even Comanches, Papa?" Ben asked.

"Them, too," Whit said. "Only most Comanches never give you much of a chance to know them. They're too busy scaring the daylights out of you."

"Bet they don't scare you!" Billy sat up and gazed at Whit. His eyes were aglow with special affection, and Whit pressed the boy's arm.

"They scare me plenty," Whit admitted. "Sometimes it's good to be scared a little. It keeps you on guard, alert. A man who gets reckless out here gets dead plenty fast."

Each day thereafter as Whit and the others worked the stock or moved the cattle along the creeks, he kept a weather eye out for trouble. The scouts resumed their spying on the house, and twice Whit saw bands of Comanches nearby, once two miles above the house along Jones Creek. The other time three Comanches chased Charlie Quinby along the Trinity before Whit and Ed broke their ranks with a pair of shells.

Then, for no reason at all, the Comanches disappeared. Not a sound was heard from Comanche Crossing, and not so much as a mockingbird feather hinted of Black Hand. Whit grew more cautious than ever, but the Comanches appeared to have swung southward to raid the farms below Fort Richardson. Then one afternoon Whit spotted a single moccasin floating in the Trinity just below the crossing.

"It didn't just grow here," Ed pronounced. "Bound to've come with a foot attached."

Sure enough, the crossing was cluttered with sign, tracks so fresh Whit could smell the horses.

"Ed, maybe you ought to ride to the fort and tell the colonel," Whit said, scratching his chin. "May just be a waste of time, but I count up to forty riders hauling along another fifty or so horses. They may want to sample our stock, too."

Ed nodded and headed his horse southward through the river toward the fort.

"Tom, you go back home, lower the shutters, see Lucy and the boys are safely inside. Charlie,"

Whit went on, turning to the younger Quinby, "let's have ourselves a look around."

"I don't have anything better to do at present," Charlie said as Tom headed for the house. "Don't plan to get me killed just yet, do you?"

"No, we've got a farm to work, Charlie."

Whit led the way westward, over a small rise and along to a place where two lodgepoles and what had once been a fine lodge covering of painted buffalo hide appeared.

"Lost this, I'd judge," Charlie suggested, gazing nervously at the surrounding trees.

"Or left it to attract our attention," Whit countered, touching the soft hide. It was as fine a piece of work as he'd encountered, and Whit felt even more uneasy. He sensed eyes on his back, but he couldn't locate their origin.

"If it's all the same to you, Whit, I'd like to get out of here," Charlie finally said. "There's something going on hereabouts."

"I know," Whit agreed, turning his horse. "But we can't panic."

"How many you figure there are?" Charlie asked as he drew his Winchester from its saddle scabbard.

"Maybe half a dozen right now," Whit said. "But there could be fifty close by."

"How close?"

"Too close," Whit warned. "Let's get clear of here!"

Even before the Comanches emerged from their wooded hiding places, Whit and Charlie were riding like fury toward the Trinity.

"Yahh-ahh-ahh!" a Comanche screamed as he hurled his lance past Charlie's shoulder. "Yahh-ahh-ahh!'' a second screamed as he threw his lance to Whit's left.

''There!'' Whit yelled, suddenly pointing to a small hill strewn with sandstone rock. ''Ride!''

Charlie noted the intensity in Whit's voice, saw the hill, then rode like a madman for its alluring slopes. Whit slowed his own pace, taunting the Indians to pull closer. But Black Hand soon appeared with twenty or thirty men, and Whit raced along to the hill.

''So, we meet again!'' Black Hand called out in excellent English. ''I have you trapped this time. You cannot get away!''

''Then come get me!'' Whit yelled as he rolled off the saddle and took out his rifle.

Whit watched in amazement as Black Hand raised his painted lance high overhead, then arranged his men in a single line that seemed to stretch forever. With a single cry, followed by a terrifying echo, the Comanches attacked.

''Lord help us,'' Charlie mumbled as the Indians surged forward.

''Amen,'' Whit said, fixing the nearest warrior in the Winchester's sights and firing. Ramming the lever down so that a second cartridge advanced into the firing chamber, Whit fired again, and again, and again.

''Lord, look at them fall,'' Charlie said, firing even as he spoke. The center of the Comanche line faltered as one horse after another lost its rider. The bright-faced youngsters at Black Hand's side lost their enthusiasm.

''Hold your fire, Charlie,'' Whit said as the warriors retreated. Soon they were swallowed by their own dust clouds. Two or three cried in pain. Others howled in grief. But most screamed threats of terrible vengeance.

"They won't make that mistake again," Charlie said, loading fresh shells into his rifle's magazine. "Let's slip on back a ways."

Whit nodded and followed Charlie to a clump of trees surrounded by a pile of rocks.

"Couldn't ask for better cover'n this," Charlie said, digging himself in behind a boulder. "Figure they'll try again?"

"Sure, only this time they'll close in slowly, try to take us from the rear. Or maybe they'll wait till dark."

"Ed'll be back before then," Charlie said, gazing southward toward the fort. "Lord, speed him on this way."

"We bloodied them some. They might give up if it doesn't prove easy."

"I wouldn't count on that, Whit," Charlie said, shaking his head. "I never knew a Comanche to give up a thing he had in his hand. No, they'll come along on."

For a few moments, though, it was as if the Comanches had disappeared. Then an arrow flew through the air, smashing into the rock just above Charlie's head. Two others followed quickly, and Whit searched to locate their firing point. Even a trained eye had difficulty spotting arrows, though, and Whit saw only shadows in the direction he looked.

Black Hand then stood up in the open, pounded his bare chest, and taunted his quarry to fire back.

"Shoot!" Charlie yelled at Whit.

"Shoot what?" Whit asked as Black Hand vanished, only to appear seconds later elsewhere.

"Shoot!" Charlie yelled again.

"If you can see him, shoot him yourself," Whit said. "You can't shoot a wisp of smoke, and that's all he is."

"He's a devil," Charlie declared.

Whit tried to calm himself as the confrontation continued. Black Hand continued to fire his taunts, as well as occasional arrows, but Whit and Charlie kept low, hugged rocks, and did their best to hide their horses.

Black Hand stood out in the open once again, shouting and goading his men to attack. Not a single young warrior went forward, and the older ones collected their horses and prepared to leave.

"They'll be here soon now," Charlie said, and Whit nodded as he watched Black Hand's eyes fill with fire. Black Hand commanded, and a dozen Comanches charged forward, weaving their way between trees, shouting and cursing and firing like the devils Charlie suspected they, in truth, were.

"Now!" Whit shouted, rising and firing rapidly at the zigzagging Indians. Trees splintered. Comanches cried out in pain. Others hugged the ground for fear of being hit.

"We showed them that time, by thunder," Charlie said as the assault faltered. "Next time, though, they'll be on top of us."

It was true. The Comanches who hadn't been discouraged or wounded lay no more than twenty feet away. Whit and Charlie would be sitting ducks if they tried to flee.

"Ever dream of how you'd die?" Whit asked. "Ever write your perfect case?"

"No," Charlie said, sighing. "You?"

"Yes," Whit admitted. "I thought it'd be at night, on a moonless summer's eve like this. I'd be holed up somewhere, desperate, trying to hold off all my enemies at once. I'd shoot three or four before they toppled me off the mountain!"

"Hero's end, some would say," Charlie commented. "But in the end, dead's dead. I'd as soon stay alive."

"Me too," Whit mumbled.

Whit readied his rifle, and Charlie did likewise. But instead of the cries of Comanches rushing ahead to avenge their dead, the clear, beautiful notes of a bugle filled the air.

"It's Ed!" Charlie cried. "We're saved!"

Whit nodded as Captain Cloud arrived, his men swinging sabers into the air and charging after the Comanches. Black Hand jumped atop a pony and fled. The others did likewise as best they could. Cavalrymen in their zest cut down a pair of Indians wounded earlier, and Whit tried not to observe the butchery too closely.

"Brought you some help," Ed said when he reached the crest of the hill. "Saved us this time, they did."

"I'm grateful," Whit told the captain.

"I told you we know how to fight this war," Captain Cloud said arrogantly. "What is the count, Corporal?"

"Twelve!" the corporal declared. "Three got themselves shot. The rest are sabered, clear as day.

All but five dead. What do we do with the ones that are left?''

''Bind them,'' Captain Cloud said. ''We'll take them back to the fort.''

''And the dead?''

''Leave them for the crows,'' the captain said, nodding to the bugler. ''We'll be pursuing now. You civilians may return to your homes where it's safe.''

''We what!'' Charlie stormed.

''We can go home,'' Whit said, pulling his companion toward their horses. ''It's over for today.''

Chapter Sixteen

Whit stood out of the way as the five captive Comanches were bound and escorted by a squad of cavalrymen back toward the fort. The remaining troopers mounted their horses and prepared to follow Captain Cloud onto the open range in pursuit of Black Hand's war party.

"We'll be hearing from that Comanche again," Charlie said, gazing at the seven corpses.

It was not a pleasant sight. The soldiers had stripped the bodies of every stitch of clothing, not to mention any ornament they happened to be wearing. Worse, several of the bodies had been slashed repeatedly by sabers.

"Souvenir hunters," Ed mumbled. "Don't suppose it matters to the dead, though."

"It'll matter to Black Hand," Whit said, staring off into the distance.

"And we'll be blamed," Charlie added.

As Whit led the way homeward, he couldn't erase the image of those seven young Comanches from his mind. The oldest might have been Tom's age, and two appeared as young as eleven or twelve. It was the war all over again, the young, eager ones charging in the front line, cut down before they had a chance to learn that the important thing about warfare was surviving. On another day Whit would have stayed behind, buried the dead. But with Black Hand on the loose, Whit fretted over Lucy and the boys.

Whit couldn't forget the bitterness he'd read in Black Hand's eyes or the cold, lifeless stare of the dead young Comanches. And in the back of his mind he envisioned other corpses — himself, Ed and Charlie, young Tom, Lucy, Billy and Ben. . . .

Whit's fingers still trembled as he splashed his way across Jones Creek and climbed the hill toward the house. Tom Morgan stood watch, cradling a long-barreled Winchester. Lucy watched Billy and Ben chase Coley Adams around the chicken coop. Chris McDermott popped out from behind the stable.

"We seem to have a lot of company," Whit said as he dismounted.

"We heard about the Comanches, Mr.

Macomb," Chris replied. "Thought you might need some help tonight."

"Half the cavalry's out here." Whit motioned to the west.

"I guess we thought maybe you'd like to have a couple of hands here who could shoot straight," Coley said, pausing in his evasion of Billy and Ben. "We may not look like much on a horse, but we can do a fair job with those rifles."

Whit walked over and greeted the two youngsters warmly. Chris seemed to grow a little each day and was closing in on six feet, while poor Coley seemed doomed to pass another year fighting to reach saddle height. Neither seemed lacking in heart.

Lucy prepared a big meal of steaks and potatoes, topped off with a rare peach pie. As they ate, Charlie narrated the day's events, and Whit sat sadly silent.

"So you expect them here next," Lucy said when Charlie finished.

"Oh, no, ma'am," Ed said quickly. "Captain Cloud's hot on their trail."

"Is he?" she asked. "No, I know better. Those Indians will lose the cavalry in the thickets, then double back."

"It's possible," Whit confessed. "But we're ready for them."

"If you were certain of that, you wouldn't look half so glum," Lucy told him. "Don't forget, Whit Macomb, I was raised on this range. I've faced Indians before. I think we've all, Billy and Ben included, earned the privilege of hearing the truth."

"The truth is, I don't know for sure what Black Hand will do." Whit shrugged his shoulders.

"What would you do, Mr. Macomb?" Coley asked, his eyes unusually bright, "if you were him?"

"I'd have some choices," Whit told them. "I could wait for the cavalry to make camp, then hit them in the dark. I might satisfy myself with stealing their horses."

"Or?" Tom asked.

"I could raid the farms here on down toward Jacksboro."

"But then you'd find yourself in the middle of two large forces," Ed pointed out. "Captain Cloud's company and the rest of Colonel Burnett's command."

"And I could always just take to the open plain, lose myself in the emptiness out west."

But though Whit had discussed the choices, he knew in his heart once Black Hand saw those young men, some of them slashed to pieces, all left for the buzzards, the Indian would fill with rage. No, the Comanches would hit someone that night, and it made sense to prepare a defense.

Whit set to work immediately preparing for an attack. An extra cask of water was brought inside, and small buckets of water were set beside the windows in case the shutters were to catch fire. Shutters were lowered and braced. Rifles already stood at the ready, but each weapon was cleaned and loaded.

Afterward Whit made a quick scout of the hillside. The moon stood high and full, giving the trees down by the creek an eerie quality. But Comanches could conceal themselves in the shadows only so long.

"More likely than not, they'll worry us half the night, then attack come first light, "Ed said. "Best mount a guard, then send the boys to sleep."

"I'll take first watch," Whit declared. "I'll wake you when it's your turn."

"Two hours on?" Ed asked.

"Make it three," Whit suggested. "You can rouse Charlie, and we'll all be up come daybreak."

"Charlie and I'll bed ourselves in the stable. That way we can watch the stock."

"Just see to it some Comanche doesn't borrow your hair. I'm short on help these days."

"I'll keep it in mind, Whit," Ed grinned.

When Whit returned to the house, he found Lucy already busy spreading out quilts for Chris and Coley upstairs. Whit got Tom to help carry the mattresses from Ben and Billy's room down to the basement.

"We going to sleep down there tonight?" Billy asked.

"I thought that'd be best," Whit explained. "With all the shutters closed, it'll get awful hot upstairs. Down here it's cooler."

Safer, too, Whit thought as he tucked the boys in. He wished Lucy would agree to stay down there, too, but she insisted on taking a station.

"I've fired a rifle more than once in my time," she exclaimed.

Once the boys were bedded down, Whit sent Tom upstairs to pass the night with his young friends. Lucy reluctantly agreed to try and sleep in the bedroom. For his own part, Whit kept the first of the watches, the longest one, from ten that night to onc in the morning.

There'd been long nights before — during the war a hundred, and afterward more than a few. But that silent summer evening as he listened to the june bugs and crickets outside and fought to detect that first shadow of a Comanche was the worst of all. The terrible loneliness was part of it. But there was mostly the dread that those few people who meant more than the world itself to him might come to harm.

Ed Quinby took over at one, but Whit found little rest that morning. Even the slightest sound stirred him to life. Once Coley rolled over against the wall upstairs, and Whit jumped to his feet. Another time a squirrel raced across the roof and brought the whole house to life.

"Worst of all's the waiting," Whit mumbled to Lucy. "I know he'll come, but when?"

"That's his strongest weapon," Lucy said, rubbing her eyes. "Now get your rest. You'll need it."

Whit finally settled into a light sleep around four, just after Ed turned the watch over to Charlie. For a time Whit's dreams filled with a parade of faceless figures, some in gray, some in blue, others bare-chested with feathers in their hair. Each bore some wound, bullets in the chest, arrows in the shoulder, saber slashes across the forehead. It was a haunting spectacle, a nightmare of violent death.

Each in turn stepped through a shrouded gate, howling in agony at some hidden image. Finally, as all the others had passed, the hidden horror stood on two feet and revealed itself. There, wearing the very homespun shirt that rested on the back of a nearby chair, stood Whitman Macomb.

Whit awoke from the nightmare soaked in his own sweat. He shook off the terror and tried to compose himself. All around him chaos seemed to be breaking out. Feet raced downstairs, and voices issued warnings. For a moment it seemed but part of the nightmare. Only when Tom Morgan burst through the door did Whit realize any of it was real.

"Charlie's seen them," Tom screamed, pulling Whit to his feet. "Comanches!"

The dream vanished. Whit blinked his eyes open, then took command. He sent Lucy upstairs to watch the far side of the house. Tom took the front right upstairs window, and Coley took the left. Chris McDermott watched the rear.

Whit himself stayed downstairs, taking a position in the empty bedroom that overlooked the chicken coop. Ed and Charlie hid inside the stable.

For several minutes Whit began to suspect a false alarm. Even a veteran Jack County Indian fighter like Charlie Quinby erred now and then. But something moved behind the coop, and the chickens clucked excitedly. Horses whinnied inside the stable, and figures darted back and forth in the faint light of almost morning.

"Down behind the hog pens, Whit!" Ed called out.

Whit fired in that direction, and a youthful voice cried out in anguish.

"There's a bunch of 'em coming up the creek!" Chris shouted from upstairs. "Maybe fifteen."

"And five or six coming up this way!" Charlie called out.

Whit recorded it all in his head and tried to make

sense of Black Hand's plan. Clearly, surprise had been hoped for. When the first intruders were discovered, Black Hand changed his mind. There would now be a charge on horseback.

Whit frowned. Attacking a stone house on horseback would prove a failure. The only true hope was starving out the occupants, and Whit had foreseen that possibility. Ample food and water were on hand.

Whit hadn't wanted another battle, especially not one so soon. There'd been too much death already, and Black Hand's attack was doomed. The Comanches would be too exposed, and even a crack marksman would have a tough time hitting anybody behind the heavy oaken shutters of the house.

And yet Black Hand came on, charging the house defiantly. Ed and Charlie laid down a heavy fire from the barn, and Whit fired steadily, methodically, from his window. Each time a shadowy figure moved, the rifle fire intensified. More often than not the target fell, rolling over in the dust, hands flailing in a desperate attempt to fend off death.

"Watch for riders!" Tom warned.

A pair of young Comanches raced their horses toward the house. Each dragged behind him a tree branch. Dust swirled in the air, blinding everyone. Other horses followed, some dashing directly toward the house until they crashed against the low stone wall in front. Comanches rolled off their saddles and advanced toward the door of the house.

"Ed, Charlie!" Whit shouted in the hope that

his old friends might be able to take the Indians from behind. But the Quinbys were kept busy by half a dozen warriors fighting to force open the stable door.

Tom and Coley kept a hot fire coming from the upstairs windows, but a few of the Comanches had already reached the front door. Though they had no success forcing either the door or the shutters, a pair of Indians fired their guns through the slots in the shutters. Lead crashed into the table and chairs in the dining room, splintered fragile glass cups and plates, ricocheted off the stone walls so that a swarm of hornets appeared to be buzzing around the parlor.

Whit found himself without targets. He backed away from the window and stared through the doorway leading to the parlor as a pair of Indians began hacking their way with axes through the heavy front door.

"I need some help down here!" Whit shouted, pulling a chest over to offer cover once the door was broken open.

"I'm coming!" Tom cried, running down the stairs as the Comanches reopened their fire from the shutters.

"Stay clear of the kitchen," Whit warned, "but watch the door. They're liable to break in."

Sure enough, an ax tore through the top hinge, and the door was battered down by the weight of three Indians. They managed only two steps inside before Whit and Tom met them with a furious volley of rapid fire. The first two slumped over the partially open door. The third managed two steps before falling dead.

In the moment of confusion which followed, Whit slipped around the side of the parlor and pulled out his revolver. He then aimed the pistol barrel point-blank at the face of the Indian firing through the left shutter and pulled the trigger. A horrible scream followed, and Whit pulled the unattended rifle through the slot in the shutter. He then fired six rapid shots at the Indians remaining beside the door. Any left unwounded retreated rapidly.

"They're done for!" Coley shouted. "Running like rabbits!"

Whit was less certain. One of the Comanches lying in the doorway pulled himself up, raised an ax, and swung it fiercely in Whit's direction. Whit only just managed to step away. Tom fired at the attacker, and the Indian fell bleeding to the floor.

"They're running, all right," Charlie called from the stable. "But a couple are staying behind."

It was an old tactic, but an effective one, Whit told himself. Just when the enemy felt confident, lowered his guard, a pair of Comanches would open fire. With luck, two or three defenders could be rapidly killed that way.

"How are you Quinbys?" Whit asked.

"Fair enough," Charlie answered. "Ed's got some splinters in his hand, and I've got an awful headache from some fool kid of a Comanche who banged me with a club, but we'll live."

"Upstairs?" Whit shouted.

"Fine, Mr. Macomb," Coley answered, his voice full of triumph. "I think Chris might be hurt, though."

"Lucy?" Whit called.

"I'm unharmed," she replied. "Young Chris is shot, but I think he'll be all right."

Whit swung the broken door open and examined the Comanches piled in the opening. There were five of them, and two more outside. None had the childish faces Whit had seen the day before. These were tough, veteran warriors, their bodies scarred and hardened. It wasn't until Whit walked out toward the coop that he saw a pair of young eyes staring lifeless at the morning sun.

"Another kid," Ed remarked, bending over to close the boy's eyes. "Look at him! Ribs sticking out! Lord, is this what we're fighting?"

"No. That is," Whit said, staring across the creek as a single warrior stood before them.

"Black Hand," Ed said, raising his rifle.

"No, wait," Whit said as the Indian dropped his shield and tore open his shirt. Slowly, deliberately, Black Hand pulled out a knife and cut shallow gashes in his chest. As blood streamed down his naked belly, Black Hand screamed an unearthly cry, then turned his lance toward Whit.

"Don't you understand, you fool Comanche?" Whit yelled back. "I can't leave. I've got nowhere else to go! This is my place!"

"No, this is MY place!" Black Hand screamed back.

"I won't leave," Whit said, walking past Ed and Charlie toward the lone Indian. "Do I have to kill you?"

The Indian gazed at Whit with a mixture of sorrow and pain, anger and regret.

So that's how it's going to be, is it? Whit said to himself. You're standing there hoping I'll kill you.

It's a brave death, but I won't give it to you. You can still ride off.

It was as if Black Hand understood Whit's unspoken words. Two young Comanches rode over to him, leading a riderless horse. Black Hand picked up his shield and mounted the animal. Then the three Indians rode off to the west.

"You should've shot him, Whit," Charlie whispered. "He's not going away."

"I know," Whit answered. "But it's hard to explain. It'd be like shooting the last wolf, the last rattlesnake. There ought to be something left."

"It doesn't work that way," Ed argued, plucking the first of some fifty splinters from his left hand. "In this country there's only room for the strongest. The other's got to leave or die off."

"Yeah, I know," Whit said sadly. "But for all the pain and death that man's brought, I won't shoot him when he's got his shield dropped."

"Truth is, he's too much like you." Charlie slapped Whit on the back. "Like old Whit Macomb trying to fight a gentleman's war up at Vicksburg when the truth is you fight a man to win, to get it over with."

Whit nodded, but he knew there was much more to it than that. Much more.

Chapter Seventeen

With Black Hand's departure, the battle was over. Now it was time to pick up the pieces, mend the wounded, and repair the damage, as Whit had done so often before. By the time he'd returned to the house, Lucy was already busy opening the shutters so that the morning breezes could clear the heavy-hanging powder smoke from the small rooms. Billy and Ben picked up slivers of shattered glass and china. Whit climbed the stairs to inspect the damage done to young Chris McDermott.

From the look of his shirt, anyone would have thought the boy dead for sure. An arrow had somehow managed to slip through the narrow slit in the shutter, deflect off Chris's rifle, and strike the boy's left collarbone. The arrowhead pierced the skin before striking the bone, and the wound had bled steadily.

"I broke off the arrow," Coley Adams explained, shivering slightly as he soaked Chris's forehead with a wet rag. "But the arrowhead . . ."

"Yes." Whit touched Coley's arm to steady the boy's nerves. "Go downstairs and tell Mrs. Macomb I need her oil lamp and the sharpest knife she can find."

"Yes, sir." Coley raced out of the bare room toward the stairs, leaving the rag on Chris's forehead.

"Well, how are you feeling, Chris?" Whit asked, kneeling beside the fifteen-year-old.

"I've felt better," Chris moaned.

"I'll be taking the arrowhead out. You're lucky. If it hadn't been for your rifle, it might have hit full force."

"I don't feel any too lucky just now," Chris answered, fighting hard to force a smile onto his face. "I'm not going to die, am I?"

"Rest easy," Whit said, easing the boy onto the floor. "I know what I'm about. I just want to clean you up a bit now. Sure do hate to tear a good shirt, though."

"I'll buy another with my cattle money," Chris whispered.

Whit took out his knife and ripped open the bloody shirt. He then cut it away so that he could get a better look at the wound. Aside from the bleeding, the collarbone appeared to be chipped.

"How does it look?" Chris asked.

"Like you're going to spend some time in bed. Lord, what a boy will go through to get out of rounding up cattle!"

"You took a bullet out of Scotty once."

"I did, at that. Got himself shot in the hand. Wasn't much to it, though."

"Not like this, huh?"

"Well, you remember Scotty. He was always finding himself in the wrong place at the wrong time."

"You were there when he died, too, weren't you, Mr. Macomb?"

"He was a good friend," Whit sighed. "You remind me an awful lot of him, Chris. The way you ride, that stubborn streak of yours that gets you in fixes like this when another man'd be safe at home."

"Scotty always said a man should stick by his friends," Chris said sadly.

"It's not a bad way to live, Chris. Some men never do learn what it takes to have a good life. Some learn at fifteen."

"I'll be sixteen pretty soon."

"Sure, you will." Whit heard Coley's footsteps on the stairs. "You're growing like a prairie fire. Any day now you'll start sporting a beard."

"No, Mama won't have that."

"Well, if you wanted, I meant." Whit took the lamp and set it a foot or so away where the light fell on Chris's chest.

"How's he appear?" Coley asked.

"Well enough. Want to stay?" Whit asked as he ran the blade of the knife Lucy'd sent under the flame.

"He'd stay if it was me," Coley answered.

"Then in a minute I want you to hold his arms down. Close your eyes if you have to, but don't let him squirm, not while I'm cutting."

"Yes, sir." Coley took a deep breath.

"It's not too deep," Whit told Chris. "The pain won't be a lot worse, but I'm going to give you a rag to bite on. Don't bite your tongue, son. And try not to move about."

Chris blinked away a tear and prepared himself. Whit said a silent prayer, then held the shaft of the arrow with his left hand and probed for the point with the knife. As he cut deeper, Whit heard Chris muffle a cry, then pass out. Once the boy was unconscious, Whit quickly cut the point out of the collarbone, then removed a small bone chip. The arrow slid neatly out, and Whit set it aside.

"You got it." Coley relaxed.

Whit took a deep breath and passed the knife back under the flame. When the blade grew blacker, Whit pressed the knife against the swollen, bleeding wound. The sickly smell of burning flesh filled the room, and Coley grew pale. But when Whit finished, the wound appeared to have sealed itself neatly.

"Will he be all right now?" Coley asked.

"Sure. He's got a broken collarbone, and he's lost some blood. But he'll mend. Boys do that well."

Coley smiled, and Whit set about cleaning up Chris's bloody chest. Lucy sent Tom up with some clean bandages, and Whit dressed the wound, then tied down Chris's arm so the collarbone would be kept still.

"Think you can clean up this mess, Coley?" Whit asked, pointing to the bloodstained floor and the pile of brass casings from the rifle.

"Sure," Coley said.

Cradling Chris's thin body, Whit stepped toward the stairs. Carrying Chris seemed so terribly familiar, like an act he had performed a hundred times before. And as he set the boy's body on the empty bed in Tom's room, Whit couldn't escape feeling oddly protective of young Chris, of Tom and Coley, even as he did toward Billy and Ben.

Lucy, meanwhile, had gotten the splinters out of Ed's hand and found a cool towel for Charlie's head.

"This door's pretty well finished." Tom pointed to the splintered planks and wrecked hinges. "Maybe we ought to get one made of iron like they've got at the bank."

"No, we'll just make ourselves another one out of oak," Whit said. "It did a fair job. Where'd you take the bodies?"

"We spread them out on the porch," Ed replied, adding, "Best get them buried before it gets too warm."

"Yes," Whit agreed. "Maybe you feel up to digging a hole, Tom?"

"Sure," Tom volunteered. "One hole for all of them?"

"It's how we did it in the army," Whit explained. "We don't know who they are. I figure they won't mind being with each other."

"Might ought to wait till the soldiers see them," Charlie warned. "They may have their own plans."

"I won't have them stripped like those yesterday," Whit declared. "And they'll have to go through me to dig them up! Those men fought bravely. If I knew what to say over them, I'd say it. But things being as they are, I can at least see them laid safely in the ground."

Tom and the Quinbys nodded their agreement, and Tom set to work digging a trench on a nearby hillside overlooking the Trinity.

Even little Coley took turns at the digging, and the grave was ready a little after midday. The Comanches were lowered into the ground as reverently as Whit knew how, and the earth was filled in.

"I think I'd like to carve them a marker sometime," Coley said as Tom outlined the grave with rocks. "Maybe I could carve an arrow on it."

"That'd be nice," Whit said. "Seems little enough of a reminder that eight men lie there."

"One of them wasn't much bigger'n me." Coley stared at his feet. "When I saw him on the porch, I couldn't help thinking it could be me there, stiff as a board, quiet as mud."

"The thing to do, Coley, is keep in mind how quickly death can come. When you do, you realize you have to spend each minute wisely. And everything you do is precious because you might not have another chance to do it later on."

Coley nodded, and Whit led the way back to the house.

On toward evening, Chris McDermott woke. Whit talked to the boy a minute or so, then turned him over to Lucy. She fed him some beef broth and stroked his head.

"Just what he needs," Charlie said, gazing through the doorway at Chris's brightening eyes. "There's no replacement for a woman's touch. There's a healing power in those soft fingers."

"Yes," Whit agreed, stepping outside and sitting on the porch. Moments later Billy and Ben sat down on either side of him. Whit unconsciously raised his arms, and the boys nestled in next to him.

"Was it bad, Papa?" Billy asked, touching a spot where blood had soaked into the wooden planks of the porch.

"Fighting's always bad, son," Whit told the boy. "People died today. There's nothing good in that."

"Chris got hurt," Ben whispered.

"Yes, and Ed Quinby, too," Whit said, softly squeezing both children. "They'll be all right, though."

"But not those Indians," Billy said. "I looked at them. They were dead."

"You know what that means?" Whit asked.

"When Papa, our first papa, I mean . . ." Billy said, his face revealing confusion, ". . . when he died, Mama and Reverend Henriks said he wasn't going to be around anymore, not so you could see him anyway. He was up in heaven watching over us. You suppose he is still, even though you're our papa now?"

"I like to think so," Whit said.

"Are all those Comanches there, too?" Billy asked, gazing up at the sky.

"Must be awful crowded," Ben said, scratching his head.

"Oh, I think there's lots of room up there," Whit said.

"What's it like?" Billy asked, shaking. "Is it like it is down here?"

"I don't know for sure, but I hope it's better," Whit said, watching clouds cross the sky. "I like to think God gives you a big old fluffy cloud to lie on, and there's no one collecting taxes or shooting guns or yelling. Everybody gets on like they're family."

"Even Comanches?" Ben asked.

"Everyone," Whit said. "I think that's what it ought to be like anyway. But I don't really know."

"I like the part about the clouds," Billy grinned.

They might have talked more, but the sound of horses splashing their way across Jones Creek drew Whit's attention.

"Ed, Charlie, Tom!" Whit called, then grabbed his rifle and trotted toward the creek. But as it happened, instead of Comanches, Whit discovered Captain Cloud's weary column riding back to the fort.

"It appears we're too late," the captain said, pointing to the Comanche bows and rifles stacked on the porch and the obvious signs of a struggle.

"Black Hand gave you the slip again, huh?" Whit asked. "Well, I could've told you he'd come back here. He's one tricky Indian. You can rely on him to do the most unreasonable thing."

"I gather you didn't kill him," Captain Cloud replied. "Get any of his men?"

"Don't you want to know if we're all right?" Tom asked.

"All in good time," the captain said. "First, the Indians."

"Eight dead we know of," Whit answered. "Some wounded. I'd estimate there were maybe thirty of them."

"We spotted tracks of at least fifty or sixty," Sergeant Douglas said. "I'd say you must have caught a splinter group. Could be Black Hand'll be back now he's reinforced."

"Maybe," Whit said, not really believing it. Eight men were too many to lose raiding a single farm.

"We're following Black Hand right now. He appears to be headed toward the fort."

"What?" Whit asked. "I watched him ride east. I'd guess he's camped up on Turkey Creek. It's an old Comanche gathering spot, close to the Trinity crossings and mustang country. There's a lot of pasture and game."

"I don't understand you, Macomb," the captain remarked. "I just told you he was headed south. You seem to think you know his every step. And you'd have me believe he's a mind reader."

"There's no magic to it," Whit said as he shook his head. "You're easy to predict, Captain. Black Hand, well, he's lost some good men the past couple of days, so now he'll lay low and let those still alive rest up. His ponies are tired, too. As to south, there's nothing there to tempt him. The grass is no better, and the towns are bigger, better protected."

"Well, I don't agree with you in the least," Captain Cloud declared. "I mean to keep on Black Hand's tail, hound him till he faces my men in battle. Then we'll solve this problem once and for all by killing that Comanche."

Whit just shook his head. He did extend what comforts he could to the soldiers, though. Buckets of cool water were drawn from the well, and the wounded were given refuge for the night in Whit's stable.

Whit wanted to convince the captain to spare his command a long pointless ride to the south, but Captain Cloud refused to listen. So the troopers headed out on their exhausted animals, their earlier eagerness long swallowed by the long, hard ride.

Chapter Eighteen

The following morning Whit rode to Fort Richardson to report the conflict to Colonel Burnett. Whit was amazed to discover that the series of hovels on the far bank of Lost Creek had grown into a smaller version of The Flat, a little town dubiously named Sudsville.

"Strange name," Hannah McDermott told Whit. "Nothing clean about that place!"

Whit passed on news of Chris's wound, and Hannah promised a visit that evening.

At the fort, Whit spoke with a tired Colonel Burnett.

"We send out patrol after patrol, but they never turn up a hair. It's hard to engage a ghost in combat! We ought to be able to treat with them, persuade them to give up the warpath and settle down to reservation life."

"Some did," Whit explained. "In the late fifties there was a reservation up on the Clear Creek of the Brazos, another one spread south from Fort Belknap. But the government didn't give them a chance. They finally marched all the Indians north of the Red River."

"It's where they'll end up sooner or later."

"Some won't," Whit said sadly. "Too many Comanches would rather die first. Many are doing just that."

Whit went on to speak of the events of those past two days, the youngsters who'd shown such bravery in rushing to the attack, the determined Black Hand baring his chest before Whit's rifle. He read none of Captain Cloud's cold-blooded desire to kill Indians in the colonel's eyes.

"What we really need to solve this problem, Macomb," the colonel said, "are guides who know the country, men who can seek out and destroy the Comanche camps, hit him in his lair, so to speak."

"That would help," Whit agreed.

"Interested in the job? Doesn't pay much, but it'd be in your interest to have this Comanche problem tended to."

"I've got a job," Whit explained. "I've got a wife and two boys, another child on the way, and I have to look after their needs first."

"Of course." Colonel Burnett smiled. "If you have any further sightings, do let me know. There's always the chance we may have someone more competent than Captain Cloud to send."

With his business at the fort completed, Whit mounted his horse and made his way back to the farm. The rest of that day and most of the next were spent replacing the door and getting Chris McDermott back on his feet. Then, after scouting the crossing for signs of Comanches, Whit collected Tom and Coley and set off down Jones Creek to hunt wild hogs.

"I would have thought you'd used that rifle enough this week," Lucy complained before they left.

"None of us'll mind the fresh meat," Whit told her, "and just now I think I need a little ride."

"And the boys?" she asked, pointing to Tom and Coley.

"I thought to send a side of bacon to Coley's mama and some chops to Hannah. Chris will be going home soon."

"I don't suppose the Adams clan would turn away food," Lucy sighed. "Maybe they'll get Coley fed a little, take a bit of the vinegar out of his disposition."

Whit nodded. In truth he knew it was little Coley's bluster that endeared the boy to everyone.

As it turned out, the hunt was soon interrupted by the passage of Captain Cloud's company, all one hundred of them riding in a perfect column of twos. The captain ignored Whit and continued leading the formation out toward Turkey Creek.

"Too late to catch him there now," Whit commented. "No, Black Hand won't be keeping to his camp anymore. He'll be rounding up his men, getting ready to fight."

Sergeant Douglas and three troopers served as scouts for the column. The sergeant left his men long enough to join Whit on the hillside overlooking Turkey Creek's third bend.

"Never saw a sign of Comanches down south. You were right about Black Hand doubling back."

"That captain needs to learn his enemy. It isn't the first time old Black Hand tried that."

"Captain Cloud needs to learn lots of things," Sergeant Douglas retorted. "Like leading a column without flank riders into hostile territory. Truth is, he's so eager for a fight he doesn't much care how many of us get ourselves killed in the process."

"Watch youself, Al," Whit said, feeling closer to the grizzled old cavalryman than ever.

"Know any prayers for a man riding through the valley of death, Whit?"

"Only the psalm. But I might be able to keep you out of ambush. Got a map?"

The sergeant pulled a chart from his breast pocket, and Whit examined it carefully.

"You call this a map?" Whit asked, staring in disbelief at the piece of white paper marked only by a few blue lines, a black circle representing Jacksboro, and a star for Fort Richardson.

"I'll bet you could fill in some of the blank spaces," Sergeant Douglas pleaded.

"Most of them," Whit said as he climbed off his horse and made his way to a large boulder. The sergeant dismounted and followed. Whit began pointing out features, and Sergeant Douglas took a quill from his dispatch case, dipped it in a small ink jar, and began filling in the hills and creeks of Jack County.

"Just ahead of you," Whit said, pointing to a ridge, "is Silver Hill. Between there and the east bank of the creek the plain narrows considerably. It's a fine place to jump a column."

"And to the west?"

"Is where I surprised Black Hand last fall, took the horses. The ridge there's too high. But if he could catch you at the creek, with Silver Hill to hide his riders, he could do a fine job of cutting you up."

"Any other likely danger spots?"

"Well, Black Hand could hide fifty to sixty men in any of these arroyos. But at least you'll have a hint he's there, and he can't hit you from more than one side. It's in this ridge country you're in the most danger."

"I know," the sergeant agreed. "But that's where the captain plans to take us."

"I hope you don't get the whole command shot to pieces," Whit warned.

"How would you do it if you were in charge?"

"I'm not," Whit said firmly.

"But if you were?"

"I'd organize my command into squads, spread out till we found Black Hand's camp. Then I'd pull the command together and hit hard."

"I'll keep that in mind. Captain Cloud and his lieutenant ride smack in front of everybody. Could be they'll catch the first volley."

"I wish you luck." Whit passed the map back to the sergeant. "Looks as if you'll need it."

"Would appear so."

As the sergeant rode back to rejoin the scouts, Whit waved for Tom to take the lead. A pair of porkers were spotted and were shot immediately. Whit noticed the boys lacked enthusiasm, though, and as they tied the animals behind their horses for the ride back home, Whit knew their feelings.

"Yanks or no, I hate to see them riding out there like that," Coley remarked. "Suicide."

"I was hoping Corporal Hodges might give me another music lesson," Tom added. "He's right in the front group there. Black Hand'll have him dead by nightfall."

"Black Hand could be halfway to the Brazos by now." Whit tried to relieve the boys' fear.

"You don't believe that, Mr. Macomb," Coley said. "Neither do we."

None of them felt a bit better when the echo of gunfire rolled down Turkey Creek a half hour later.

"We should go have a look," Coley said. "One of us at least."

"No," Whit said. "Even all three of us wouldn't be any help if they're in real trouble. And if they're not, the captain would only resent it. Best thing to do is get this food home, ready the farm in case Black Hand rides through tonight."

Whit quickened the pace, and the youngsters reluctantly followed. It was as hard a thing as Whit had ever done, riding away from the noise of desperate battle. His mind filled with images of Al Douglas fighting for his life, trying to rally the cavalrymen along the banks of Turkey Creek. But

Whit believed what he'd said to Tom and Coley. The cavalry had its job, and Whit had his.

The gunfire died down as Whit wove his way through the post oaks that grew thick along Jones Creek. The battle was drawing to a close, and whatever had happened was history. By the time Whit, Tom, and Coley rode up to the stone house, the rolling range behind them was as silent as midnight.

"I see you got your hogs." Lucy smiled at them. "We heard you shooting."

"That wasn't us, ma'am," Coley said as he slid off his horse. "The cavalry's having a go at the Comanches up Turkey Creek."

"That right, Whit?" Ed asked, wrinkles appearing on his forehead.

"Sure is," Whit told them. "After the meat's dressed, we'd better ready ourselves for more trouble."

"It always comes, doesn't it?" Charlie grumbled.

After the hogs were butchered, Lucy prepared a wonderful meal of pork chops and onions, boiled potatoes and green beans. As she spooned portions of peach cobbler onto empty plates, someone shouted outside.

"What was that?" Billy asked, jumping to his feet.

"I'll take a look." Whit motioned for Billy to sit down.

"I'm coming with you," Tom declared.

The two of them grabbed their rifles and started toward the edge of Jones Creek. The sun was already settling into the hills to the west, and the creek bottom had become a mass of distorted shadows. It took several minutes to pick out the bedraggled figure of Pat Hodges from his surroundings.

"Corporal Hodges!" Tom yelled, racing to the young soldier's side. "What happened?"

"My horse took a tumble a couple of miles back," the corporal said, leaning against a willow and trying to muster strength. "Had to walk the rest of the way."

"We'll get you to the house," Whit promised. "That ankle looks to be troubling you."

"I think it's broken," Corporal Hodges said. "The sergeant put me on the best horse we had left, but the ground's so full of holes, and I'm not the ablest rider."

"Tell me what happened," Whit said, supporting the corporal's weight. "We heard the shooting."

"I have to tell the colonel," Hodges mumbled. "We need help."

"I'll send a rider," Whit pledged. "Now, what happened?"

"Sergeant said you guessed it. We were moving along the creek when we came to three fallen trees. Lieutenant Ames was having them cleared when Comanches hit our rear and flanks. Then more of the devils opened up from the hillside. Before we knew it, the command was cut to pieces. Over twenty dead. Maybe twice that wounded. All the horses and pack mules run off."

"I'll ride to the fort," Tom volunteered.

"No, I'll send . . ."

"I'm going," Tom declared. "I can ride as fast

as anybody, and I'm not needed here. All I have to do is follow the road."

Whit reluctantly nodded his agreement, and Tom raced off toward the stable. Whit then helped the corporal up the hill and on to the house.

"Well, what did you expect from that ironheaded captain?" Whit asked as he led Corporal Hodges to a chair. "Lucy, fetch some bandages."

"That ankle's broken," Ed declared. "They get the whole company?"

"Most are pinned down along the creek," Hodges explained. "They're low on ammunition, and it's getting dark."

"I wouldn't want to be them," Charlie said, sadly shaking his head. "Did Tom go to the fort?"

"Yes," Whit told them. "Now, let's see what we can do for this man. Best prepare for others, too."

Chapter Nineteen

It was near midnight when Tom returned, his shirt soaked through with sweat, his face ashen from exertion. Colonel Burnett stopped by briefly to speak with Corporal Hodges, then led his relief force on toward Turkey Creek and Captain Cloud's shattered column.

Whit kept two guards posted all night, but no Comanches appeared. By dawn the Trinity echoed with the sound of supply wagons banging their wheels on the rocky road. But the first trace of Cloud's survivors wasn't to be spotted for hours.

"It's worse than I dreamed," Whit admitted as wagon after wagon of wounded crossed Jones Creek and headed for the Buffalo Springs road. Even those still breathing had the lifeless eyes of the vanquished. Those strong enough to drive the wagons were little better. Pat Hodges, wearing splints on his shattered leg, hobbled to the porch to search for comrades.

"When's the sergeant coming?" Hodges asked the last wagon.

"He's already gone by," the driver answered. "Right in front, with Lieutenant Ames."

"Dead?" Hodges asked, shaking so violently Whit feared the young man might fall.

"Drove off the final charge, but caught a lance for his efforts," the driver explained.

Whit walked out and helped the corporal sit on the porch.

"No, Mr. Macomb, I ought to be on that last wagon," the corporal argued. "With the sergeant dead, it's my duty."

"I'll have Tom drive you in later," Whit said. "You can't do any of those boys any good."

"It's Cloud's fault!" the corporal said bitterly, slamming his fist against the planks of the porch. "Sergeant warned him. There never was a better man born than Al Douglas. Was like a father to me. Isn't right."

Moments later Colonel Burnett appeared. Beside him rode the very same Captain Cloud, his uniform slightly wrinkled, but otherwise none the worse for the ordeal.

"I'll shoot him!" Hodges declared, searching the porch for a weapon.

"Ease up, Corporal." Whit frowned. "I knew

the sergeant a little myself. He wouldn't like that."

"You don't understand," Hodges said, tears appearing in his eyes. "We thought Cloud was dead. He just lay there as the rest of us were being shot all to pieces."

"Could've been unconscious," Whit suggested.

"You don't believe that, and neither do I," Hodges mocked. "I'll see he's rewarded for this."

"No, you won't," Whit said sadly. "All you'll do is bring trouble on yourself. If the captain's to be punished, it'll be Colonel Burnett's doing."

Hodges struck the porch again, then nodded.

Colonel Burnett turned away from the ragged train and rode toward Whit. Captain Cloud, his face as pale and shallow as his men's, rode onward toward the fort.

"Got time for a walk?" the colonel asked.

"Sure," Whit agreed as Colonel Burnett climbed down from the saddle.

They made their way through the thickets past the stable and on out to a small knoll overlooking the creek.

"I guess you know what's happened," the colonel said, slapping his knee. "Never has the Sixth taken a beating like this! I've got twenty-four men to bury, and five or six likely to lose limbs. Out of a hundred men, there are twenty uninjured, and they won't be fit for duty anytime soon."

"I understand Sergeant Douglas was killed." Whit tried to keep his voice calm. "He was a good man."

"One of the best. It's that fool Cloud's fault, of course, though he'll likely be played for a hero by the newspapers. The thing is, we've got to put an end to this. From your report and the figures Captain Cloud provided, this Black Hand can't have but thirty or so men left. He's on the run. We've got to strike now, catch him while he's worn out."

"And before he makes use of all the guns and ammunition he picked up last night," Whit said nervously.

"Exactly. Citizens don't take kindly to being massacred by Springfield rifles they had to pay for."

"You hardly needed to discuss any of this with me." Whit stared off down the creek.

"Yes, I did. Because I need a scout, a man who knows this country like the back of his hand, a man who's fought Comanches, knows their thinking."

"I told you," Whit reminded the colonel, "I've got a job."

"I did you a favor arranging horse and cattle contracts. An even bigger one getting your steers to Kansas. Matter of fact, I've got a bank draft back at the fort for you."

"I don't get the money unless I take you to Black Hand. Is that the offer?"

"No, the money's yours," Colonel Burnett said. "I only mean I've helped you through a tight spot. Now I need you to get me through one."

"I suppose I do owe you," Whit admitted. "But I've got a wife and . . ."

"Talk to her. But consider this: We'll never have a better chance to end these raids. And you'll never build a real future here until the Comanche menace is removed."

Whit nodded.

"We'll head out early tomorrow morning," declared the colonel as Whit led the way back toward the house.

"I'll speak with Lucy," he answered. "Till then I can't make any promises."

Lucy, as could have been expected, was far from delighted with the colonel's offer.

"You have responsibilities," she reminded Whit. "Billy and Ben. Not to mention the little one right here," she added, placing Whit's hand on her swollen belly. "I need you, Whit. Even good men, the kind who know what they're doing, get killed in a battle."

"I know," he agreed. "But I owe the colonel, Lucy. More than that, I owe you a chance to lead your life without being scared that a howling wolf might really be a band of Comanches out to kill us all."

That night as they lay side by side in bed, the night filled with eerie shouts and haunting bird whistles. Wolves howled like never before, and Lucy sat up each time Whit awoke.

"Do what you have to do," she finally told him. "Only don't forget what's waiting for you here. Don't throw it away, Whit. We need you so much."

"And I need you," he told her.

Colonel Burnett arrived a half hour after sunrise, leading a reinforced company of the Sixth Cavalry on the best horses left to the command. There were no supply wagons, no pack train. It was clearly a strike force, bent on catching Black Hand quickly and dealing with the Comanche once and for all.

"You'll look after Lucy and the boys, won't you, Ed?" Whit asked as he saddled his horse.

"Fine time to ask that." Ed grasped Whit's hand firmly. "See you watch out for yourself. Those bluecoats won't take care of you like the Second Texas did."

Whit led his horse out of the stable. Billy and Ben sat beside the chicken coop, quietly watching. Whit dropped the reins and trotted to them.

"Seems like we ought to be good at good-byes by now," Whit said, shaking each small hand in turn. "But I don't suppose a man ever . . ."

"We know, Papa," Billy said, wrapping his hands around Whit's leg. "We'll be fine."

"And I'll be back soon," Whit added, kneeling down so that he could dry a tear streaking across Ben's small face.

"Wish I was big enough to go with you," Billy said, hiding his face so Whit could not see the tears dripping from his eyes. "I will be pretty soon."

"You mind your mama, and see she doesn't work too hard," Whit told them. "Won't be long before you have a little sister to look after, too."

"Or a brother," Ben insisted.

Whit turned back to his horse, pausing only once to glance back at Lucy. They'd said their farewell words before breakfast, and he couldn't bear another good-bye. Tom Morgan waved, and Whit nodded his answer. Then Whit Macomb, old soldier that he was, climbed into the saddle and headed out on what he hoped would be the last campaign, the final battle of a strife-torn life.

All I ever hope to have, he thought, *is waiting for me back there. Lord, now all I want is a little peace so I can live out my days with them.*

"So," Colonel Burnett said when Whit arrived,

"I thought we'd send the main column north toward Buffalo Springs. Then we can swing back west and south, trapping Black Hand along one of these creeks."

The colonel pointed to the rough lines on the map Whit had drawn for Sergeant Douglas.

"They'll read your dust for miles," Whit explained. "No, first you've got to lose your men in the post oaks. Then we'll send a party to locate Black Hand. Along the way we can clear Silver Hill of scouts. It's as good a lookout as Squaw Mountain. Once we find the camp, you can use your West Point strategy."

"Fair enough." The Colonel waved his soldiers around as Whit led the way northward along Jones Creek. In an hour the whole command vanished into the oak forest. Whit found himself heading out with five troopers toward Silver Hill.

"You sure this is the way to do it?" a thin-faced corporal named Magruder asked. "This is the place Al Douglas got himself killed, isn't it?"

"No," Whit said, "and I don't plan to get any of us dead. We'll come up the back side, then catch anybody who's on top by surprise. If I'm right, Black Hand's camp won't be far away."

As they rode, Whit felt strangely haunted. He'd ridden those creek bottoms with his brother Marty what now seemed like a hundred years ago. They'd swum and fished every inch of the place. And before too long more men were going to die for those wild, unsettled acres that had always belonged as much to the wind as to any man.

It's not enough to write words on a deed of ownership, Whit thought as they began the climb up Silver Hill. There'd never really been any silver there, of course, but once . . .

Whit's mind cleared as he spotted an Indian pony. He motioned for the troopers to stop, then slid off the chestnut stallion and drew out his knife. The others did likewise except for a single man left to guard the horses.

"The first one," Whit whispered, pointing to a slightly built young Comanche sitting atop a limestone boulder. The corporal waved, and a trooper cautiously stepped forward, then grabbed the boy from behind. The Comanche kicked twice, then grew silent as the soldier's knife plunged downward.

Whit turned away as the trooper tore a necklace from the young man's chest. Souvenir hunting was all too common in the Dakotas. Comanches were fond of wearing blue tunics in winter, making medallions out of watches, even cutting rings off fingers. Mutilation was rarer, and Whit was relieved the trooper's knife, once cleaned, had been returned to its scabbard.

The other scouts, three of them, watched the valley intently, laughing as they told stories of previous deeds. Whit spread out the soldiers, leaving the corporal to assign each man a target. Whit chose to cut off any retreat. The cavalrymen lurched forward, and the scout on the left was cut down almost immediately. The one in the center fended off his attacker, then drove a knife into the belly of the bearded bluecoat. The corporal clubbed the right-hand scout, then went for the sole remaining warrior.

"Get him, Bob," the trooper on the left called out.

Whit motioned for silence as the corporal squared off with his enemy. Whit raced over and inspected the unconscious boy on the right. Boy he was, no older than Tom, and Whit quickly bound the small hands with a rawhide strip cut from the boy's own leggings. Whit likewise bound the boy's feet, then stuffed a piece of shirt into his mouth.

The corporal and the Comanche scout still turned half circles around each other. Finally the Indian made a lunge, and the corporal opened up a terrible gash across the Comanche's belly. The wounded scout stared down at his open wound, sang softly a death chant, then stumbled off the edge of Silver Hill and tumbled to a quick death below.

"Once we find the camp, you can send this one back," Whit said, pointing to the bound boy.

"Better to kill him and have done with it," one soldier argued.

"He can't be fourteen," Whit said, lifting the Comanche's head so the soldiers could see.

"I had friends with Captain Cloud," the corporal said.

"Me too," Whit said, staring hard at the trooper. "But that doesn't make me a butcher."

Whit made his way along the crest of Silver Hill, reading the landscape below. He finally saw what he sought high up on on Turkey Creek. Light wisps of smoke rose from campfires. A dozen makeshift lodges had been constructed from government blankets. Sunlight flashed off rifle barrels stacked beside cartridge boxes.

"There," Whit said, pointing it out. "We'll go on ahead and scout the camp, Corporal. Leave two men here to keep watch. The other can take this Comanche back to the colonel and order the column forward."

It was as Whit and the corporal started down Silver Hill that the old uneasiness returned. Any minute a party of Comanches might appear. Two men alone had scant chance.

But Black Hand appeared satisfied with scouts on Silver Hill. Why shouldn't he be? Whit asked himself. Up to that point the cavalry had proven itself a poor opponent.

Black Hand's camp on the east bank of Turkey Creek was a mile and a half north of the spot where Whit had raided the horse herd. Between lay the shambles of Captain Cloud's disaster — dead horses and spilled provision sacks, cavalry hats and pistol belts, shredded clothing and discarded weapons.

The camp itself was a lively place. Young Comanches romped through the shallow creek, singing their victory songs and waving stolen blankets in the air. Others wore soldier tunics and hats as they ate slices of roasted beef, no doubt a cow with the WM brand. Whit counted thirty men, maybe more, with a few youngsters thrown in. Close to another twenty wounded lay on blankets beside the creek.

Whit and the corporal watched the camp for better than an hour, all the while fearing each Comanche glancing eastward would detect their presence.

But the camp remained as it was until Colonel Burnett led the balance of the troops past Silver Hill.

Whit sat with the colonel in the sand and sketched the camp. The colonel studied the picture, then called his officers over.

"Captain Hanford, you're to take forty men and come down from the northwest, across the creek. See no one escapes that way," commanded the colonel.

"Captain Stoneman, I want you to strike from the southeast with another forty men. Hit them hard, Captain. I want them fleeing when Captain Hanford's force appears."

"Yes, sir."

"The balance of the men will form a line around the camp. Lieutenant Glass, that will be your post. As the bugle is blown, I want a steady fire directed at those Indians. Understand?"

"Yes, sir."

"We strike in a half hour, gentlemen. Don't be late," the colonel warned.

The officers set about assembling their separate forces, and Whit stood beside the colonel. Any minute the sound of a horse whinnying or a soldier cursing might alert the camp. But to Whit's surprise, no one in the Comanche camp seemed concerned about anything more serious than a race through the creek.

It's strange, Whit thought as he saw the pieces of Colonel Burnett's plan come together. Whit knew he should feel glad, should eagerly await the slaughter. But it was like the night before they'd hit the Yanks at Shiloh. The vision of so much death staggered a man.

The bugles blasted, and the riflemen surrounding the camp let loose a volley. Lodges were torn apart, and Comanches cried out in pain. It was worse than anything Whit could have imagined. As Captain Stoneman's column charged forward, those wounded who could move fought to get to their feet. The others scrambled to find their rifles. Black Hand emerged from one of the lodges, shouted at his companions, then began forming a thin line along the creek.

The cavalrymen left their horses and crept forward in pairs, firing rapidly. But Black Hand's warriors hid behind trees, rocks, dead horses, anything that would provide cover. The Indians soon began picking off the lead soldiers of Stoneman's command. Only the wounded Comanches, unable to get to cover, continued to die.

Black Hand was everywhere, rushing to the aid of the wounded, rallying his warriors. For a while it appeared that the Comanches might be able to escape across the creek. Then Captain Hanford's troopers surged into the shallows, shouting and firing wildly. Their appearance seemed to stun Black Hand, take the life out of his face.

But not for long. There was something about desperation that lent strength to a man. Hanford's troopers were halted across the creek, and each one that attempted to splash through the water was quickly cut down.

"He's retiring toward those willows," Whit explained to Colonel Burnett. "Once there, you'll never catch them, not with your horses running wild all over the place. A Comanche on horseback is gone!"

The colonel rode off to reinforce the riflemen on the right, but Black Hand remained a step ahead. He gathered his men and charged the thin line of bluecoats. The Comanches shouted and screamed, and the troopers fell back.

"Get after them!" Colonel Burnett shouted.

But though Captain Hanford and a dozen horsemen hurried to cross Turkey Creek and cut off the Comanches, the bigger part of Black Hand's little party escaped. But not their leader. Black Hand would not leave the others. Instead, he and three companions wove their way back to the creek, where a half dozen Indians tried to withstand the withering fire of Colonel Burnett's riflemen.

It was all but over. The Comanches could not hold off the ever-encroaching bluecoat marksmen. One after another, the Indians fell.

"Can't you see they're finished?" Whit asked the colonel. "Hold your fire. Ask them to give up."

"Cease fire!" the colonel ordered. "Cease fire."

The riflemen continued firing, relenting only gradually. When the rifle fire finally stopped, Colonel Burnett called out in a loud voice, "Drop your weapons and step out. We will not fire on you!"

Black Hand stood in response, but he didn't drop his rifle.

"You have no chance of escaping!" Colonel Burnett shouted. "Give up!"

Black Hand glanced at his companions. Most were already bleeding from more than one wound.

"Save yourselves!" Whit called out.

Black Hand glared at the surrounding cavalrymen, then looked straight at Whit. The Indian's face grew solemn, and he nodded. Then, shouting loudly, Black Hand charged straight for the colonel. He got within ten feet before a dozen bullets shattered his chest.

Whit sighed as the other Comanches followed their leader. The troopers shot each in turn, though toward the end Whit noticed a reluctance as the rifles were leveled and fired.

When the last of the Indians had grown still, Whit followed the colonel through the maze of death and destruction. The soldiers inspected each corpse in turn, stripping the bodies of clothing and jewelry, sometimes kicking at their former enemies with hatred. But Whit thought he caught glimpses of respect from many of the veterans.

"Captain Stoneman!" Colonel Burnett called out.

The captain trotted over on his horse, and the colonel issued orders to send messengers to the fort for wagons. Another party was assigned the task of burying the dead Comanches, all save Black Hand, who was to be taken to the fort.

As the burial details set to work, Whit wiped the sweat from his forehead and set off homeward. What was it Al Douglas had said — the valley of death? Yes, that was it exactly. And it would take a lifetime to erase the stain of blood from the land.

Chapter Twenty

Whit wandered across the land, seemingly without direction or purpose. It should have been the best of times. Black Hand was dead, and those Comanches who had escaped the terrible onslaught on Turkey Creek would pose no threat to the struggling farms of Jack County. But with the passing of the Comanche threat came the passing of a time, and such a passing required at least one mourner.

As he rode the tree-dotted hills and the muddy creeks that were Macomb land, that had been for most of Whit's lifetime and would be so long as

Macombs cared to have it so, his mind filled with a hundred memories. There were solemn, tearful moments like the burying of the dead or grief for fallen friends. There were days of laughter spent chasing Marty through the streams and hours spent sharing quiet moments with Lucy or helping the boys to understand the baffling world they were growing to discover. It was a good place to be. It was home.

Whit finally rode up to the house toward sunset. Lucy stood in the doorway, tears streaking down her face as she watched him climb down from his horse.

"It is over now?" she asked.

"Black Hand is dead," he told her. "And he's the last of his kind."

She clasped his hands, and Whit pulled her close.

The following morning Steve McDermott rode out to invite the whole crew to a celebration in Jacksboro. Entire steers were being barbecued, and mounds of potatoes and yams were being baked. The bakery at Fort Richardson would provide the bread, and some of the Sudsville saloons were donating cider.

"Do you feel up to the trip?" Whit asked, touching Lucy's stomach. "Time's nearly here."

"I won't miss the only party we're apt to see in a year's time," she answered.

So they set about seeing to it that everyone had a bath and clean clothes. Lucy put on her best bonnet and had pails of milk and a tub of butter placed in the back of the buggy. She then took her place beside Whit. The boys slid in back with the milk and butter, and Whit started toward town.

By midafternoon Jacksboro was alive with

celebrating. Soldiers and townsfolk cheered each other. Only the tent women from Sudsville weren't welcomed.

Most of the people seemed to be gathering around the steps of the courthouse, and after driving the buggy around to the back of the Stratton House, Whit made his way over there. To his horror Whit saw an undertaker had laid out Black Hand in a wooden coffin. The Indian's eyes had been pried open so that they glared at their enemies, and the bullets that had torn into the Comanche's chest had left it bruised and broken.

"Who did this?" Whit demanded to know.

"Ease up there, Macomb," Judge Baker said. "I'd think you'd enjoy seeing him as much as anybody."

Whit stared angrily at the judge, then marched off down the street. He finally found an equally glum Ruben at the stable.

"It's a poor end for a brave man," Whit complained bitterly.

"It's the times, Whit," Ruben sighed. "Don't spoil the party for yourself. Go along, have some fun."

"No, I don't feel like celebrating. For all the trials I've been through, he played the game by the rules, the same way we've always fought and died out here. This — well, it's something from the outside, and it doesn't belong. He should've come to a better end than this."

"He's dead now. He doesn't feel any of it."

"I suppose you're right. Still . . ."

"It was always them or us, son. You know that. Their time had come."

"I wonder how long it will be before our time comes." Whit stared at the far horizon. "Doesn't seem like the range'll ever run out of cattle, that the creek could dry up, or that the sun could stop shining. But . . ."

"Whit, no man ever decided what's to be. The best he can do is get by, do right by his family and his friends. As for the plains, well, I hear out beyond the Clear Fork a man can walk a hundred miles on buffalo bones. That's what'll kill off the Comanches, the Kiowas, all the plains tribes. I recall the time when you could stand beside Lost Creek and see nothing but prairie grasses and post oaks. That's changed, Whit, but I have to think it's for the better."

"Maybe," Whit admitted.

"Now, why don't you run along to the party? Can't have a young buck like you spending all his time with a bald old cuss like me."

"All right," Whit agreed, nodding a farewell to Ruben.

The parlor of the Stratton House was alive with laughter. Hannah McDermott passed a platter of food around, and Chris filled cups with cider.

"Oh, there you are, Whit Macomb," Hannah said, setting her tray aside and motioning for Whit to follow.

"Have you seen Lucy?" Whit asked.

"Everyone's seen Lucy except you." Hannah rested her hands on her hips. "Do you know what's happening?"

"What?" Whit asked as she pulled him along down the hall.

"Why, only the most important thing that can

ever happen," Hannah declared. "She's down in my room bringing your baby into the world."

"What?"

"You heard me."

"But . . . how? I thought . . ."

"You men." Hannah shook her head. "You think you can plan on when a child comes into the world! Fools, every single one of you."

"So, where are the boys?"

"Across the hall." She pointed to the open door of the smaller bedroom Chris and Steve shared.

Whit bolted down the hall. The sounds of Lucy moaning and groaning in Hannah's room drew him to her, but old Mrs. Lattimore raised her hand to halt him.

"Can't you tell what we're about, Whit Macomb?" the old woman asked. "This is women's work. You stay clear!"

Whit started to object, but Lucy screamed, and he retreated hurriedly.

"It won't be long now," Hannah told him. "Why don't you go wait with the little ones."

Whit nodded and stepped through the door into the other room.

"Why the glum looks?" Whit asked as he sat beside Billy and Ben on the bed. "You'd think you boys were sick!"

"Is Mama going to die?" Billy asked, clutching Whit's arm. "She's hurting awful bad."

"Well, boys, it hurts bringing a baby into the world," Whit explained.

"Was it like that when I was born, too?" Ben asked.

"More than likely worse, you being such a lively

type," Whit said, laughing. "Thought about what you want to name her?"

"Her?" Billy said, frowning.

"Don't you want a sister?"

The boys frowned awfully, and Whit laughed.

"Girls aren't so bad. Your mama was one once," Whit told them. But neither boy seemed convinced.

Tom entered the room then, handing out glasses of mint tea and biscuits.

"You have any sisters, Tom?" Billy asked.

"Had one once," Tom answered. "Real sweet little thing. Annie was her name. The Indians got her."

"I guess a sister wouldn't be too bad," Billy said, looking at his brother. "We could name her Harriet, after the cow we used to have."

"You can't name a baby for a cow," Tom said, laughing.

Whit laughed, too, then left the boys to argue about the names. He knocked on the door across the hall, then stepped inside.

"I was just going to get you," Hannah said from the bedside. "There's someone here who wants to see you."

Whit leaned over the bed and kissed Lucy's forehead. He then took a peek at the small, wrinkled baby wrapped in a cloth at Lucy's side.

"The boys are thinking of names," Whit whispered. "Harriet seems to be the favorite."

"Oh, that will never do." Lucy smiled, fighting the fatigue. "I was thinking about Whitman, or perhaps Ruben."

"Don't you mean Ruth?" he asked.

"No, I'm afraid I've brought you another boy," Lucy said. "I don't suppose you'll mind too much."

"No," he said, touching the baby's chin. "I know a pair of ranch hands who'll be relieved."

"But next time it better be a girl," she declared.

Whit kissed her again, then stepped across the hall to tell the boys. Billy and Ben raised such a shout you'd have thought the Comanches had returned.

Later that evening, as the celebrating in town ebbed, Whit took a long, solitary walk along the banks of Lost Creek. A new moon drifted in and out of the clouds overhead, and Whit found himself smiling.

A new moon? It was fitting. It had been a day of birth, of new life rising amid death.

To think they call this place Lost Creek, Whit mused. It seemed a strange name for a place where he'd found so much.

Yes, he thought as he gazed at the moon. A new moon was appropriate for a new beginning. With that in mind, he turned back toward the Stratton House, toward Lucy and the new little son who would draw them even closer together.